I0623201

THE LOTUS FOUNTAIN

Published in Canada by Engen Books, St. John's, NL.

ISBN-13: 978-1-989473-89-4

Copyright © 2020 Engen Books Ltd.

The fictional world 'Lotus Lorea ' presented in this novella and all original characters and concepts presented thereon are copyright © 2020 by Nicole Little.

Cassidy Cane, Herbert Gamgee, Tallis, and all other original characters and concepts presented in this novella are copyright © 2020 by Matthew LeDrew.

NO PART OF THIS BOOK MAY BE REPRODUCED OR TRANSMITTED IN ANY FORM OR BY ANY MEANS, ELECTRONIC OR MECHANICAL, INCLUDING PHOTOCOPYING AND RECORDING, OR BY ANY INFORMATION STORAGE OR RETRIEVAL SYSTEM WITHOUT WRITTEN PERMISSION FROM THE AUTHOR, EXCEPT FOR BRIEF PASSAGES QUOTED IN A REVIEW.

This book is a work of fiction. Names, characters, places and incidents are products of the author's imagination or are used fictitiously. Any resemblance to actual events or locales or persons living or dead is entirely coincidental.

Distributed by:
Engen Books
www.engenbooks.com
submissions@engenbooks.com

First mass market paperback printing: November 2020

Cover Design: Ellen Curtis

Slipstreamers Committee:
Amanda Labonté
Ali House
AJ Ryan
Ellen Curtis
Erin Vance
Lauralana Dunne
Matthew LeDrew

THE LOTUS FOUNTAIN

NICOLE LITTE & JD RYOT

BOOKS

CHAPTER ONE

"Have they been located?"
"Yes, ma'am."
"I expected as much. Thank you."
"And, what of the visitor?"
"It's been… taken care of."

Boom.

***

The first sentence is always the most difficult one to write, she assured herself, *just give yourself a few minutes, you'll figure it out.* And yet there she sat (it had been inevitable of course) for endless moments, irrevocably stumped, tapping a pen against her lips, staring at that blank white piece of paper. She needed something clever but it also had to be heartfelt and sweet; something eloquent but not too formal.

She sighed.

Words. What were those again?

Congratulations! Cassidy finally wrote in desperation as the hands on the clock ticked by at an alarming rate. She chewed thoughtfully on the top of her pen for a moment and then, when nothing else came to her, she scrawled *Best wishes, Cassidy* at the bottom. There. Perfect. Or, at least, as good as it was going to get. She tossed the pen onto the desk where it disappeared amongst papers and folders, half full coffee cups, and general office flotsam. She crammed the card into its envelope and placed it inside the gift bag, atop the brightly coloured tissue paper. Hidden amongst the folds of canary yellow was a tiny t-shirt emblazoned with the phrase *Archaeology—I dig it.* It made Cassidy chuckle. Okay, sure she had rolled her eyes at first. It was a tad bit silly, but it began to grow on her as she had frantically searched, and came up otherwise empty handed, for a suitable present in the university gift shop.

A baby shower. It was a first for Cassidy Cane. She was wearing (and she couldn't quite believe it herself) a dress. Her hair was freshly curled and fell in soft waves that brushed against her shoulders. Her hands itched to haul it up into its usual ponytail.

The party was being held in one of the University's many function rooms, the organization of which had been delegated to a lowly research assistant in the Anthropology Department. Tables had been pushed to the sides of the room and chairs were lined up against the walls. Three blue and white balloons were tied to a podium; a hand written sign, taped on the wall beside the door read:

Welcome

Mateo Romero-Jones

to the Plainsfield Family!

Cassidy's eyes widened and she let out a low whistle.

Wow. Clearly they had spared no expense on the decorations.

Cassidy heard laughter and the low rumble of intimate conversation as she approached the room. She stood in the door way, hesitating. A few professors that she recognized from her own department were milling about inside, as well as a number of others that she did not know. Gamgee had been right to insist that she attend, of course. Between travel and work, her social status at the University, and well, if she was willing to admit it, her social status everywhere else, was at an all time low.

With a sigh, she stepped through the doorway.

Lars Economides from English waved a sandwich at her from the refreshment table; he held a red solo cup steady in his other hand. She was quite glad he hadn't tried to wave with that one. Lars was a bit of a klutz and he was wearing a light-coloured leisure suit. Etienne-Andre Durand, French Department, nodded politely when he caught her eye. He then glanced at his watch and resumed tapping his foot.

Annie Jones grinned in delight when she spotted Cassidy from across the room; she waved a hand and beckoned for Cassidy to come closer. Annie's wife, Ximena Romero, was cradling a blue bundle, her smile content as she swayed to and fro in a slow, rhythmic but gentle motion.

"I am so glad you are here, Cassidy! Meet Mateo!" Annie beamed with pride, gesturing toward her new son. "I haven't had a full night's sleep in what seems like forever but who needs sleep anyways, right?!"

Cassidy laughed. "I'm so happy for you both!"

"Thank you! We are just over the moon!"

"Dr. Gamgee sends his regrets. He's at home with a bit of a head cold today. He didn't want to pass it along to the baby, but he hopes to meet Mateo soon!"

"Of course! We completely understand. Please tell him we hope he gets well soon," Annie replied.

A tiny head dusted with wispy strands of raven hair poked out the top of the soft blanket in Ximena's arms. Cassidy peeked inside. Cocooned within, Mateo yawned and stretched laboriously, one tiny hand escaping its woolly confines. He blinked up at her. His dark, unfocused eyes were adorned with impossibly long lashes. They dominated his heart shaped, dusky-pink baby face.

"Adorable!" Cassidy exclaimed, and truly meant it.

***

Within the hour, the celebration was in full swing; the number of people in the room had increased exponentially. Someone from the Spanish Department had snuck in several bottles of wine and another, a middle aged man with a bright green Mohawk, had hooked a phone up to a small speaker, which had, inexplicably, started pumping out instrumental covers of theme songs from popular television sitcoms. A few ladies were dancing. Somehow baby Mateo was sleeping through all the ruckus.

Cassidy balanced a paper plate of assorted sandwiches and small cookies on her knee. She'd retreated to a far corner where she could sit and eat in peace. And to observe, of course. She liked to watch people in their natural habitats, to attempt to interpret their body language, to read their facial expressions; to try and figure them out—who they really were beneath the mask of social constructs.

Huh. So maybe *that* was why she didn't have very many friends. She'd have to give that a bit more thought later, when she was relaxed at home and fully prepared to psychoanalyze herself.

Hunger satiated for now, Cassidy left her plate on the chair to mark her spot and went in search of a drink at the refreshment table. She skirted around several small groups of people, clustered together in conversation, excusing herself as she stepped in front of them and around them. What a crowd! Had strangers just wandered in off the street? She wedged herself into the small space between the table and the wall, a small alcove created by the storage room door, and was pouring herself a glass of tepid lemonade into what she hoped was a clean cup, when a snippet of half-whispered conversation caught her ear.

"… us that we were the perfect candidates and just a few days later we had a call saying that our file had been chosen by one of their clients. By the end of the week, we were bringing Mateo home!" Annie's voice was low but animated.

Cassidy inched a little closer, keeping her back to the two women who were huddled together chatting quietly. She pretended to be looking for a napkin, while in reality she was eavesdropping with complete and utter abandon.

"Incredible! I have friends who have waited *years* for that call!" came the hushed reply.

"We were very lucky! We had to sign a non-disclosure agreement, if you can believe it. I probably shouldn't even be discussing this in public," she giggled and then continued, the wine clearly having loosened her tongue, "The amount of paperwork was just astronomical. Totally worth it of course, don't get me wrong! Rising Sun have truly made our dreams come true. We're just not supposed to tell anyone the details!"

Cassidy pleaded exhaustion and said her goodbyes shortly afterwards, once more congratulating Annie and Ximena on the adoption of their son before she left. If she was being honest, and Cassidy was often brutally so, she simply wanted to go home and ruminate on what she had just overheard.

She also desperately wanted to shed the dress.

Once home, she quickly changed into more comfortable clothing, some old sweatpants and a favourite but faded shirt from an 80's hair band. She plopped onto the couch and reached for her laptop, sliding it onto her legs and powering it on. The startup prompted her for a password; within seconds she'd clicked into the main screen of a popular search engine. Fingers flying, she typed *Rising Sun Adoption* into the box, hit enter, and waited for the results to populate.

Nothing.

Cassidy drummed her fingers on the arm of the couch. She typed *adoption agencies near me*. Again, no results.

Curiouser and curiouser by the minute. And like a dog with a bone, Cassidy was *not* letting it go.

Cassidy glanced at the time. It was late but not *that* late. She nibbled on a thumbnail and then, before she could change her mind, she grabbed her cell.

The phone rang once at Cassidy's end before Gamgee answered with, "Good evening, Cassidy!"

"Good evening, Doctor. I hope you are feeling better. I was wondering if I could ask you a quick question?"

"Not feeling too bad for an old man with a cold, I suppose!" he replied in a nasal voice. "And, of course, you may ask me anything! I trust you enjoyed yourself at the baby shower?"

"Ah, you bet! I sure did," Cassidy fibbed.

Gamgee chuckled, then coughed. "I am glad that you decided to go. Now, to what do I owe this pleasant surprise?"

"Well, I was wondering, have you ever heard of a Rising Sun Adoption Agency?"

He paused. "No, I don't believe I have. It doesn't sound familiar anyways, sorry."

"Oh, that's too bad. I was just—"

"Wait!" he interrupted. "Now that I think about it, it does sound a little bit familiar. Could it be The Rising *Son* Agency?"

"Oh! Yes! It might be! I may have just misheard."

Gamgee made a noncommittal noise and finally: "It's near my place but at the other end of Carina Heights, up in the old gated community, I believe. I rarely drive over that way; they're horribly slack with repairs you know. The roads are terrible. I've heard rumours there's even a big gap in their security fence. Imagine!" He sounded horrified at the thought.

"Yes, of course, that is quite unfortunate. I'm sorry to have bothered you when you're under the weather, curiosity got the better of me I'm afraid. Perhaps I will follow up in the morning."

"You know what they say, Cassidy: there is no time

like the present! Hope you enjoy the rest of your night."

"Thanks, Doctor G. You too."

Cassidy chewed absently on her lower lip, and glanced at the time again. Her hunch that something was *off* about the whole situation was sitting heavy in the pit of her stomach. And her gut had never led her astray before. Well, maybe a few times. Before she could change her mind, she'd run into her room to change her clothes. Moving with urgency, for reasons she could not quite explain even to herself, she grabbed her keys, pocketed her phone and hurried out the door.

She'd worry about the gates when she got there.

Locks had never stopped her before.

CHAPTER TWO

The crunch of gravel beneath the tires was reminiscent of the cracking of long buried bones as Cassidy pulled up as close as she dared to the closed, and presumably guarded, gates of Carina Heights. She left the car in a pool of darkness in between street lights and beneath a no parking sign she did not even acknowledge. She pulled a dark stocking cap low on her head and eased the door shut with a muffled click. Slipping around the side of a faded but once elegant welcome sign, breath misting in front of her face, she cringed reflexively as the crunch of leaves and the snap of twigs beneath her feet rang out like a shot in the night. She froze. Heart pounding frantically, yet in a way that she still strangely enjoyed, Cassidy paused only for a moment, and then plunged headlong into the darkness.

Gap in the fence. Was that right?

Cassidy ran, glancing over her shoulder frequently before she finally stopped to catch her breath. She could see lights off in the distance, not too far at all. She moved up close against the fence, following along the length of it. She crept by, hand trailing against the chain links. This was taking far longer than she had anticipated. But she was committed now.

Finally, there it was: the gap in the fence just as Gamgee had mentioned in that offhand way of his. Invigorated now with this convenient discovery, Cassidy rushed forward. She cursed elaborately as her jacket snagged on a jagged bit of fencing. Cassidy gritted her teeth and gripped the material, ripping herself free. Chastened, she now made sure to step carefully through the hole. Directly in front of her and across a plush, expansive lawn was a large squat building—and coming down the street in front of it was the flash of oncoming headlights! *Dammit!* She would be caught for sure. Cassidy's mind quickly calculated the list of criminal charges she had amassed thus far tonight. Not good. Not good at all. Crouching low, she made a dash for the cover of the darkened exterior of the building. She flattened herself against the back wall just as a private security vehicle drove slowly past. She needed cover. *Now.* Pulse quickening, Cassidy reached up behind her and, to her surprise, discovered that the window slid open easily. When no alarm immediately sounded, she hoisted herself to the ledge and dropped inside, feet first. She slid the window closed behind her and allowed an audible breath of relief to escape her lips.

She grinned. She was safe.

At least for now.

But that was all that really mattered.

Cassidy waited for her eyes to adjust to the too dark darkness. She couldn't risk using the flashlight on her phone. Too much light would make her much too noticeable, especially with security skulking around. Briefly, she wondered just what the hell she was doing here. But the thought was fleeting, swallowed up by the giddiness and thrill of the chase. She did this sort of thing all the time right? Slowly, shapes in the room came into focus. She was in someone's office. There was a desk, a chair, and filing cabinets. She picked her way gingerly across the room and towards the desk, slow going, taking her time in the unfamiliar surroundings. A cracked shin was something she did not need right now. Cassidy reached for her phone, deciding she would risk using the dull backlight of the main screen to illuminate the paperwork upon the rich mahogany surface. *The Rising Son Adoption Agency* read the letterhead.

Oh. Heck. Yeah.

Delighted, feeling as though lady luck was by her side tonight, Cassidy felt emboldened enough to leave that particular office and explore further in the building. The adjacent wall in the hallway outside the door was adorned with simple black picture frames that held photos of cheerful happy babies. Successful adoptees, Cassidy presumed. She tried the door across the hall only to find it was locked. As was the next one. The third door opened into a small kitchen. It was of little interest to her—she did not care to learn what their preferred brand of coffee was or how many tubs of expired yogurt the fridge held. By the time she had reached her fourth locked door in succession, Cassidy felt her frustration reach a pinnacle. Trespassing or not, she wasn't leaving without some kind of answer to the questions that had plagued her all night. But so far, she wasn't getting anywhere.

She very much did not want to go home right now. Especially since she had come this far. And broken so many laws. In pursuit of what exactly though, she wasn't sure. Just that feeling in her gut. Something was up.

Cassidy's eyes alighted on a door at the end of the hall. Like a moth to a flame, her attention was immediately drawn to the glow of a keypad. Security such as that usually meant that there was something behind the door that was worth hiding. So her hunch had been right after all. Her excitement mounting, Cassidy strutted boldly up to the door. It was a numbered keypad, simple for the most part, but how many attempts would she be allowed to try before it locked her out? There could be thousands of possible combinations. Suddenly she stifled a snort of laughter. Written in light pencil, just to the right of the keypad: 1015. Cassidy punched in the number and grinned in delight as the lock disengaged with a soft click. Things were going a lot easier than she'd imagined.

Maybe it was even a little too easy?

A buzz ran up her arm as her fingers lightly touched the doorknob and Cassidy flinched in surprise. What the hell was that? She wrapped her hand around the knob, turned and pushed. Before she was even fully in the room, she felt the thrumming along her veins, the pressure in her ears, that had, over the last little while, become so familiar to her. So intoxicating. But no. *It couldn't be? Could it?!* Brazen now, Cassidy felt along the walls nearest the door and, finding exactly what her fingers sought, she flipped the switch, flooding the room with a dim florescent light. She gasped.

How was this even possible?

She took a step forward, hesitated, not quite sure if she could believe her eyes.

Sure, she'd expected to find *something* inside The Rising Son Adoption Agency but she certainly hadn't expected that something would be a portal.

CHAPTER THREE

Cassidy shook her head as if physically trying to dislodge the image in front of her. It remained solid. She was not normally given to flights of fancy, it was true (and she knew it), but she was still reassured to know that she was not just imagining things. She took a step forward, her brow furrowed; her brain running a mile a minute.

"There's no one here, boss."

Cassidy jumped.

A crackle of static: someone was nearby. She moved closer to the door, straining to hear. "I checked all the offices. No signs of break and enter." More static, a mumble of words, then: "I'll make one more round. Something must have tripped it."

Dammit. There must have been a silent alarm after all. Cassidy cursed again beneath her breath. Such a stupid, rookie mistake. If the guard came any closer down the hall, he'd notice the open door; for certain he'd notice that the light was on. Cassidy wondered if she would have enough time to ease the door shut; if there would be time to hide.

The sound of approaching footsteps, then an excited:

"I think I've got something boss!"

Cassidy considered her limited options, but really there had only been one viable option all along. Even if there *had* been other options, the look on her face suggested she would not have chosen them anyways. A mixture of excitement and anticipation flushed her cheeks and she grinned widely.

"Here we go again!" she murmured under her breath.

As the guard began to step hesitantly through the door, Taser extended forward in a shaking hand, Cassidy turned her back on him and launched herself forward. She heard him shout "STOP!" in a nervous, quavering voice, but there was no stopping now. She plunged through the portal at a dead run.

Immediately, Cassidy wished she *could* stop. Momentum carried her forward into a tumble, a riot of colours blurred past her, and then the crushing impact as she hit the ground, bounced, rolled and then landed face first. She grimaced in pain as her right hand took the brunt of the skid; she felt a snap; heard a muffled crack, then, warm and sticky, blood began to flow freely and plentifully from a gash that spread across her palm. Cassidy clutched it protectively to her chest as she lay, winded, upon the uncomfortable uneven ground. Sound came back to her all in a rush and she could hear several timid voices speaking uncertainly around her. Someone was screaming.

Oh. Wait. That was her.

"Clear the way, children, please. Let me through now!"

This was not a hidden portal. No one seemed surprised to see someone come through either.

Beneath her eyelashes Cassidy saw the shadow of a figure walk forward and crouch down next to her, speaking urgently and with authority: "Are you able to get up?"

Cassidy gave a brief nod and, teeth clenched, was helped to her feet. Her left hand shading her eyes in the bright sunlight she blinked rapidly at the sight before her. A woman wearing a long flowing dress and a flower crown stepped forward, her salt and pepper hair nearly to her waist.

Was she dead?

"Well, this is not how we normally treat our visitors," the woman gestured towards Cassidy's injured hand and smiled. "But all the same, welcome to Lotus Lorea!"

No. Not dead.

"Thank you," Cassidy said, hesitantly sounding out the words, her speech slow and slurred from shock and pain. They spoke English here. Or at least this woman did, though it was with a slight accent; lyrical and pleasing to the ear.

"You've no need to be afraid, child. You are safe here with us. My name is Marcella; please, let us take care of that hand for you."

Cassidy glanced down and saw that the clothes she had changed into before leaving her house were saturated in blood. Her hand throbbed in time to the rhythm of her heartbeat. This wasn't her first injury and she was certain it would not be her last either, but she reckoned there was no reason why she should just stand there and bleed to death. She nodded her consent.

"Eliza, please bring some water from the fountain to the infirmary." A small tow-headed child sprinted away, clearly elated to have been chosen for this special task.

"Come along with me, Cassidy. I am sure we can find something clean for you to wear as well."

Feeling lightheaded, Cassidy heard herself mumble, "How did you know my name?"

"Oh, I am sure you mentioned it, dear."

And that was all Cassidy heard before everything faded to black.

***

Cassidy regained consciousness slowly, her world coming back into focus little by little. She was flat on her back beneath crisp white sheets, her head cradled atop a soft, fluffy pillow. She blinked several times, her vision still cloudy. A light breeze ruffled the sheer curtains in the window across the room. The scent of lilac drifted in, reminding Cassidy briefly of her grandmother. She could hear the voices of children outside, laughter and the low murmur of conversation between adults.

Lotus Lorea. That was what the woman had said, right? Marcella. Cassidy was sure that was her name. Her memories of her arrival were fuzzy and distorted.

Woozy, head still spinning, Cassidy relaxed back against the pillow. She squinted in the bright light as she took in her surroundings. The room was small but neat and tidy. That familiar antiseptic smell that assaulted her senses confirmed her suspicions that she was still in the infirmary.

Then, suddenly, she remembered! Her hand! She withdrew it from beneath the blankets and found it wrapped in a long length of gauze; it was thick and stiff with the bulk of a bandage beneath. Cautiously, she flexed her fingers and found that the pain was minimal. She was relieved. From what she had seen of it, from what she had *heard* of it, and combined with the significant blood loss, she had expected much, *much* worse.

She pushed back the blankets and swung her feet off the bed. She took her time, taking deep breaths. She did not want to faint and hurt herself again. These people would think she was some kind of klutz. She glanced down at herself in surprise. She was clothed in a long billowy garment much like the one Marcella had been wearing. Underneath that, she was wearing a pair of light-weight leggings. She saw that her boots, hat, and jacket were stacked neatly on a nearby chair. Her phone had been placed on top of the pile. She quickly hauled on the boots and picked up her phone. The screen had cracked from side to side. She sighed. Another one bites the dust. She knew there'd be no point in turning it on anyways since cell phones never worked within the worlds she travelled to. She left it where it was on the chair, crossing her fingers that it would work the next time she had a chance to power it on.

It was oddly quiet here. At least it was odd to Cassidy. If she'd been pressed to further describe it she might have even said it was peaceful. Cassidy noted the absence of the sounds of traffic, cars, horns or shouting. There was no construction, jackhammers or the raucous laughter of builders. There were no angry commuters, no road rage or cursing bus drivers. She couldn't deny that it was nice for a change.

There was a light knock at the door behind her. It slid open and Marcella's head appeared through the crack.

"Oh good, you are awake! How are you feeling, okay?" She beamed at Cassidy, who nodded and returned the smile. "It's nearly lunchtime. If you're feeling up to it, please come join us!"

A long table had been set up in the community centre. A simple white cloth ran the length of it. The table was laden with an impossible amount of food and Cassidy gaped in astonishment. Bowls of luscious deep violet-toned grapes, glistening trays of ripe cantaloupe and juicy pineapple; there were lychees and pomegranates, dragon fruit and papaya; parfait cups were filled with berries and clotted cream. There were several types of produce that Cassidy did not recognize and she thought, perhaps, these fruits (or whatever they were) were native to Lotus Lorea. Their diet, Cassidy couldn't help but notice, seemed entirely plant based. There were no meats in sight, though there were bowls of what appeared to be oatmeal or some type of cooked grain. Large bowls of vibrant leafy greens were placed in the centre as well as at both ends of the table; luscious tomatoes on the vine stood out next to them, begging to be sliced.

A hush fell over the crowd as they noted her arrival. The children stared wide-eyed with undisguised interest and there was an anticipation to the silence as the crowd held their breath and waited for the newcomer to do something … anything.

Cassidy felt a bit like a deer in the headlights but still she managed to smile and say hello.

They smiled back.

A few of the children waved.

"Please, won't you take a seat, Cassidy. Here, next to me, and we can have a bit of a chat."

Cassidy sat where Marcella indicated and, as if by some unspoken communication, conversation around the table resumed. The children re-commenced their bickering, and platters of food were passed around; plates were heaped high and smiles were broad and joyful. Cassidy would not have been able to guess as to the ages of those present. Wrinkled, smiling faces watched toddlers and teenagers alike with the same indulgence and tolerance; soft, creased hands patted the round bellies of several pregnant young women—eager to hold their grandchildren.

Quickly, Cassidy remembered her manners. "Thank you, Marcella. For everything you have done for me since my … unexpected arrival." She wiggled her fingers under the table, once again amazed at her recovery from what she was sure should have been a debilitating injury.

Marcella patted Cassidy on the arm gently, "It's been no trouble dear. We are glad to help when we can. I am sorry that you did not have a more pleasant welcome. Please, help yourself to some food! There is plenty for everyone!"

She didn't need to be told twice. Cassidy helped herself to everything within her reach and then to more as the platters were passed around. She was ravenous. Food had never tasted this good. A cold glass of mango juice appeared next to her plate and Cassidy drank deeply of the chilled beverage. She couldn't help but close her eyes in ecstasy. It was as though all her senses had been heightened—especially that of taste.

"What brings you to Lotus Lorea, Miss Cassidy?" a curious voice asked.

Cassidy's eyes popped back open, seeking the person to match with the voice: a child with a bright, earnest face regarded her with a friendly grin. Cassidy paused for a moment, thinking, then: "Curiosity?" she offered ambiguously.

Marcella laughed. "Well that's just as good a reason as any, now isn't it? Once you have finished eating, perhaps you would like to join me on a tour?"

"Yes, thank you! I would enjoy that very much."

The conversation flowed freely; Cassidy listened as her lunchtime companions spoke of their day and the work left to be done before night fell. As lunch came to an end, the women rose together and began to clear away. Others tended to the children; young mothers nursed infants hands-free in complicated ring sling carriers while they chased toddlers and carried empty bowls and plates. Cassidy watched in amazement. They were like a well-oiled machine.

As Marcella and Cassidy left the community centre and strolled down the cobbled streets of Lotus Lorea, a soft, fragrant wind lifted the hair from their faces; a warm caress, soft as a mother's touch.

"It's very tranquil here."

"I'm glad that you think so." Marcella beamed. "We constantly strive for calm. It takes balance and hard work. We are very much about equality and there is no class structure here. Everyone does their part; everyone chips in and helps out, especially with the children. It takes a village to raise a child, you know. If you have any questions at all, please do not be afraid to ask!"

Cassidy nodded. Marcella was really selling it but something was nagging at the back of Cassidy's mind. Annoyingly, it stayed right there, just beyond her reach, an itch she couldn't quite scratch.

"Our homes are fairly large, as you will notice," Marcella pointed out, "but they are communal. Each floor holds one family and there are several families to a house. We have a school for the younger children as well as a training centre for our graduates where they can choose to learn from a wide range of vocations and trades. We encourage a love of reading and learning from a very young age! Our children are the future … they will carry on the legacy of Lotus Lorea."

As they walked, Marcella gestured towards the cluster of homes and then the other buildings as she described each one and its purpose. They were by no means opulent but still quite impressive if for their sheer size alone. The school was a low, flat, nondescript building with bright murals painted on its facade; the training centre was attached to it by a short walkway and was quite similar, though it lacked the charm of the murals. The buildings were more functional than anything else; Marcella explained that despite their outwardly bland appearances, their training facilities inside were ultramodern with state of the art training equipment. Students there learned everything from cooking to engineering and nursing. There was also a gym and exercise centre; Cassidy noticed a yoga class schedule posted outside as they passed by.

As they drew near the large fields full of crops and plants, Marcella explain that they were completely self sufficient. They ate only what they were able to grow or make themselves. Cassidy took note of a small brick building, much closer to the wooded, undeveloped area than the residential space she was getting a tour of. Marcella did not mention it. Immediately Cassidy's curiosity was peaked.

"What's that building over there?"

Marcella paused. "Oh. That's just The Hut. Storage for gardening supplies and things like that."

They had nearly walked the entire u-shape of the village when they came upon the library. It was particularly splendid, with a gabled roof, brick façade and trailing vines that surrounded two large, carved wooden doors.

"The library is one of our more elaborate structures," Marcella announced proudly. "It is also our oldest building, having been built by the original founding members of Lotus Lorea!"

There was nothing nondescript about the library. Cassidy took it all in with wide eyes, delighted, and made a promise to herself that she would visit the library the first chance that she got.

Their outing ended in the town square. "Here we are then," Marcella remarked. "This concludes our tour! I hope you've learned a little about us and how we live and work. I am quite proud of all that we have accomplished."

She gestured towards the wide open space of the town square, and further still a small park and grassy area. Cassidy's attention was drawn to a girl who was reading contentedly, propped against the wide base of a weeping willow; a small child was flying a kite nearby. A picnic had been set up beneath the shade of a cluster of the low hanging trees.

Cassidy took it all in with a wide smile. She turned around to express her delight to Marcella but then gaped in wonder, the words dying upon her lips. In the very centre of the courtyard was the most beautiful water fountain she had ever seen. It was a solid grey concrete, smoothed with age but untarnished. It was large and impressive but somehow managed to not be overwhelming or ostentatious. In the middle of the fountain, a curved cement bowl—resting at a slight angle—was perched atop two Greek Corinthian style columns; water gurgled from within the bowl and cascaded downward in a clear, steady stream where it splashed and bubbled joyously in the pool. But the most incredible part was a small, delicately carved stone child who sat perched at the very edge of the basin, her tiny feet submerged in the water. Her hands were cupped beneath her face, her lips pursed as though she were preparing to blow a kiss; within the chalice of her hands she held a single lotus blossom in full bloom.

"This is … exquisite!" Cassidy had finally found her voice.

Marcella watched her with a knowing look. "Isn't it? We call it The Lotus Fountain."

"Incredible…" Cassidy could barely tear her eyes away from it. There was something about the fountain that was mesmerizing. She felt an inexplicable connection to it; the gentle flow of the water calmed her immediately; the statue of the child stirred feelings that she could not even explain.

This ambiance was something that many people strived to achieve in their own homes and gardens back in Cassidy's world. But they had all failed miserably in comparison to aura of The Lotus Fountain.

A squeal of laughter snapped Cassidy out of her reverie and she was catapulted back to the present. A small group of children dashed by, riotous with laughter, and as she watched them go she had a sudden moment of clarity.

"Marcella, remember how you said it was okay to ask if I had any questions?"

"Yes, of course, my dear!"

"Um … just exactly where are all the men?"

CHAPTER FOUR

Cassidy had been offered a room in what Marcella re-
ferred to as The Dorms. From what Cassidy had seen so
far, it housed mostly young women who attended the vocational school or those at the cusp of adulthood: too old
to still want to live with their family, but too young to be
with a family of their own. Of course, she had accepted.
She wasn't ready to go back home through the portal yet.
Not even close.

The room she had been given was small but functional
and, best of all, private. Cassidy was grateful for it; she
knew that she would eventually have to earn her keep,
had in fact offered to help out in whatever way she could.
But for now Marcella had told her to try to relax; to recov-
er from her fall and subsequent injury; to get used to her
new surroundings. There was a single bed placed in a corner of the room farthest from the door. It was draped in
a homemade patchwork quilt sewn with bright, cheerful
squares and threads. Two plump, down-filled pillows in
mismatched pillowcases were stacked against the head-
board. There was a lamp and a washbasin on a nearby
weathered antique bureau; a small, ornate brass mirror

hung above it. Next to the basin was a beautiful silver comb and brush set, a small hand towel and a bamboo toothbrush.

A window overlooking the fields offered natural sunlight. Cassidy squinted in the brightness, eyeing the brick building she'd noticed earlier on her tour. A myriad of mouth-watering scents wafted in through the open shutters, disrupting her line of thought. Someone was baking something that smelled absolutely delightful. Scones perhaps, or a pie. Maybe even bread. Saliva flooded Cassidy's mouth. How could she possibly be hungry after the incredible feast she had consumed at lunchtime?!

Cassidy sat on her bed and mulled over the story Marcella had shared with her in the town square. Sitting together on a well-worn wooden bench, the two women had discussed things quietly and at length. Cassidy listened intently and tried not to interrupt, though she had many, many questions. Even though the information that Marcella had imparted was common knowledge to the people of Lotus Lorea, her and Cassidy spoke together in hushed tones. Marcella's voice was reverent. Cassidy lost hers in shock.

There were no men.

Lotus Lorea was a matriarchal society; founded by women, led by women for women and those who identified as them. The children were raised together in complex family homes—mothers, sisters, aunts, cousins, grandmothers—they all lived together and shared the responsibilities of a household. No one was forced to take on traditional roles assigned to them by a male-dominated culture. There were no expectations that they would marry or bear children or uphold an outdated standard of femininity if they decided that path in life was not for them.

Marcella spoke passionately, though not zealously. She was adamant that their world had achieved nirvana. They did not *hate* men, and had much respect for them she insisted; they just chose *not* to live amongst them. And they were not welcomed on Lotus Lorea.

It was a whole lot of new information to digest all at once.

Cassidy had definitely seen pregnant women at the communal lunch and there were a great deal of children running around but, still, Cassidy hesitated to voice the obvious question.

Awkward.

She chewed on her bottom lip, concentrating, her brow furrowed in thought.

Now that she looked back over the events of the day and the people that she had met, the inviting faces who had greeted and welcomed her at lunch had indeed all been women and young girls. She hadn't put a lot of thought into it and, if she *had* given it a fleeting thought, she might had assumed that the men were off working somewhere or perhaps they ate separately. There had been a large number of babies and toddlers at the community centre as well, but they were dressed in a variety of different colours. Cassidy had made judgements based on how children were dressed back in her own world. Pink for girls or blue for boys—that was the usual. Long hair on girls, short hair on boys. It was a concept that was completely foreign here, but it was such a common thing where Cassidy had come from that she had not even clued in. She knew the difference now. It made sense.

Cassidy got to her feet and tiptoed to the window. It was quiet outside. She could see in the fields in the distance that people had gathered to work on the crops; there were many different kinds—rows and rows of fruits and vegetables; wheat and different grains. The climate here was something else that peaked Cassidy's interest and she added it to the mental list of all the things she wanted to investigate. It never seemed to get cold. Her list was getting very long.

Lotus Lorea seemed to be perfect. But Cassidy didn't usually believe in the concept of perfection. There were too many variables.

A peal of laughter reached her ears from the distance. Everyone was so happy and had such positive attitudes. She had not heard a complaint or an argument, no negative, sarcastic or snarky words had been spoken since she had arrived here. Only the children had bickered. And most of that had been good-natured.

Could this really be paradise?

***

Her clothes had been laundered. By some miracle they had been able to remove the blood stains. The rips in the knees of her pants had been mended as well. The stitch work was immaculate; from a distance it would not even be noticeable. Back home she would have just thrown all those garments in the garbage, went out and replaced them with something new. It really was such a wasteful attitude. Shaking her head ruefully, she tucked the bottoms of her pants into her boots and felt more like herself now that she was back in her own clothes. She carefully folded the borrowed dress she had been wearing and left it at the foot of her bed. She noticed that a pair of pyjamas had been kindly laid out for her on a chair next to the bed. They really had thought of everything.

Despite all of this, a seed of doubt was beginning to take root in Cassidy's mind, sprouting weeds of suspicion. It was difficult for her to take things at face value and, from her experience, when people treated you *this* well (especially strangers) there was an ulterior motive. There was something in it for them, or they expected something in return. And when they called in that favour, well, she was sure they would make it difficult for her to say no.

Keeping that in mind, she vowed to explore the town later, without a chaperone—to check a few things off that mental list she had found herself compiling.

She flexed her hand experimentally. Hardly any pain at all. Incredible.

Her first stop was, of course, the library. She was nearly salivating at the thought of all that she would find inside. Books were an escape for Cassidy when a real getaway was not possible. While her house did not hold all that many personal items (she kept most of her prized possessions in her office, where she spent most of her time), her bookshelves were packed to overflowing. She'd read all of them at least twice. The people of Lotus Lorea clearly shared this passion for the written word, for the library was one of the most spectacular that Cassidy had ever seen.

Cassidy stepped inside, the silence embracing her as it

had done in countless other libraries that she had visited. Polished wood floors led to an open concept foyer; off to the side was the circulation desk although it appeared to be unoccupied at the moment. Books, books and more books, as far as the eye could see. And even further than that perhaps, as the far corners of the library disappeared into darkness. Just exactly how big *was* this place?! It was a remarkable feat, this clever use of architecture. The building seemed to go on forever inside while, at the same time, outside it did not appear to take up all that much space at all.

The familiar musty smell of ink and paper flooded her senses the further she walked into the building. She breathed deeply.

With time on her hands and no place that she needed to be, Cassidy wandered the stacks unhurriedly. She'd yet to see another person. Libraries back home were bustling; someone was always shushing someone else for making too much noise or arguing with them that they were hoarding too many books. This was an entirely new concept, this silence and calm. She approached the curved staircase that lead to the mezzanine. Running her hand along the ornate craftsmanship of the timeworn but smooth and polished railing, she put her foot on the first step and—

"Can I help you?"

Cassidy gasped aloud and nearly fell over the step. She placed a shaky hand over her pounding heart and … laughed. What was this feeling? This lightness bubbling inside her chest? She turned around, a grin spreading across her face.

"Oh! I am so sorry, my dear, I didn't mean to startle

you!"

"It's okay! I just didn't notice you there."

The woman smiled.

So *this* was the librarian. And was she ever a cliché. She was older, though Cassidy would have been hesitant to try and venture a guess on her age; she could have been anywhere from sixty to eighty years old. She was grey-haired and softly wrinkled, the lines around her eyes and mouth were deep and enviable, for laughter must have come second nature to this woman. She wore half moon spectacles that were attached by a chain lest they fall and break or so that she didn't misplace them. She wore a floral dress, and a light lace cardigan was draped across her shoulders; her shoes were sensible and appropriate for someone who likely spent a lot of time on her feet, finding books or putting returns back on the shelves.

"Can I help you find something, dear?" she repeated. She glanced at Cassidy's bandaged hand. News travelled fast in Lotus Lorea. It reminded Cassidy a lot of a small town. Everyone knew everybody else, so newcomers stood out like a sore thumb. No pun intended.

"I was just having a look around. Browsing your collection. I hope that's okay. Your library is incredible!"

"Isn't it?! Or at least I think so anyways! I have worked here for 47 years this spring so I may be slightly biased." She chucked. "My name is Virginia but everyone calls me Miss Ginny—the young, the old, even Doctors. That's what they all call me! Now, you take all the time you want to look around. I must ask though that you not enter the restricted section. It contains some rather… sensitive works. It's at the back of the library, near the reference books.

You would probably walk right on past it …if you weren't looking for it." She turned and began to walk away.

"Thank you?" Cassidy called quietly, perplexed.

The septuagenarian paused in her stride and then glanced back over her shoulder at Cassidy. "I'll be taking a break for the next thirty minutes or so, just grabbing a cup of tea and a scone. I trust that you will be able to keep yourself occupied?"

Her rubber soles squeaked as she walked away across the polished floors.

Did she just wink at me? Cassidy wondered.

CHAPTER FIVE

RESTRICTED.

The sign was attached to a thick rope which cordoned off the bookstacks at the back of the library. The area behind the rope was unlit; what lay beyond, saturated in a murky darkness.

Despite the pleasant temperature inside the building, Cassidy felt goosebumps rise upon her flesh.

She glanced around.

Alone again.

She ran her hand along the rope. It was rough, her bandage snagging in the bristles. She pulled it free and then threw one leg over, casually, then the other, the way she did most things: like she belonged there; like she owned the place.

A small flashlight sat innocently on a reading table.

Surprised but pleased at the timely discovery, she turned it on and panned it around the area.

The temperature was cooler behind the rope, as though heat would dare not risk encroaching the barrier for fear of angering Miss Ginny. Cassidy blinked several times, waiting for her eyes to adjust to the dimness. The flash-

light illuminated only a short distance in front of her before the light was swallowed up by the gloom. There were
wall-to-wall bookcases and each one was packed tightly
with similarly sized volumes. The musty smell was more
intense, leading her to believe that she was most likely
surrounded by aged and, perhaps, very significant books
in the history of Lotus Lorea. She stepped up to a shelf
and gazed in awe. These books were ancient. She ran her
fingers along the spines reverently, respectfully. A thick
layer of dust coated the shelf and the books. No one had
been in here for a long time.

Holding her breath, she peered closer to take a look at
the titles, the gold words faded and worn:

Founding Mothers: A Walk Through Herstory
The Book of Sons
Letters Concerning the Gateway
Provenance and The Font

Pay dirt. But where to begin? Cassidy began to gently pull *Letters Concerning the Gateway* from the shelf. She
didn't want to damage the old book so she took her time.
Her heart was thumping excitedly—could the *Gateway* in
this title be, in fact, the portal? It made sense. The slim
hardcover was halfway out of its space when Cassidy felt
a familiar tingle in her nose. She held her breath, turned
away from the light, but it was no use. Pressure built up
in her sinuses and then Cassidy let loose with a dramatic
sequence of sneezes—her usual ten in a row. Dust stirred
up from the violent exhalation of air and Cassidy sneezed
again and again. She let go of the book and tucked her
head in the corner of her arm to stifle the noise. The fit
of sneezing now finally over, Cassidy eagerly reached for

the book once again, her fingers pulled it forward and then—

"Cassidy?! Was that you? Are you back there?"

Dammit.

(What? Were you expecting a secret passageway or something?)

She pushed the book back in place, quickly turned off the flashlight, and nimbly hopped back over the rope. By the time Marcella had made her way to the inner sanctum of the library, Cassidy was sitting at a reading table far, far away from the restricted area, casually flipping through the pages of a book on tinctures, poultices and herbal remedies.

"Oh, there you are, Cassidy! One of the community elders said they saw you come in here."

Cassidy smiled pleasantly, though behind those curved lips she was gritting her teeth, silently cursing up a storm in her head. She'd been *that* close. "Yes, I love old buildings like this, and especially libraries. You just never know what you might find."

A flash of confusion and what might have been mild annoyance crossed Marcella's face but then quickly cleared. Cassidy wondered if perhaps she had imagined it. Her suspicious nature and all.

"That's so very true! Would you care to join us for afternoon break? I believe one of the girls has brewed some fresh *jaroot*, if you would like a cup!"

Cassidy accompanied Marcella to the community centre; she made agreeable noises and laughed or demurred at the appropriate times in the conversation but the wheels in her head were turning frantically. She munched on a lemon poppy seed biscuit; the *jaroot* Marcella had spoken of appeared to be the Lotus Lorea version of coffee. It was served piping hot and sweet, with a dash of rice milk. The constant flow of food and drink to her mouth was an excellent excuse for not joining in the chatter with the other women.

Soon, she tuned out the noise in the room, lost completely in her own thoughts.

Miss Ginny had most certainly wanted her to find *something* in the restricted section. But what exactly?

Cassidy was going to find out, even if it meant breaking all the rules.

And she was very good at that.

***

When evening arrived, as dusk began to fall, the chime of a bell rang out. Everyone stopped working, or studying; the children put away their playthings. They all gathered in the great community hall to take dinner together, as was the custom for all their meals. A large tureen of a thick and creamy wild rice and mushroom soup was centre stage; a rich, golden cauliflower and chickpea curry took up space next to it, surrounded by an abundance of other fragrant dishes: fritters made of lentils and potatoes, an entrée of stewed tomatoes, red beans and rice. In amongst all these other dishes were pots of different steamed vegetables; one that was similar to eggplant but the colour blue, another of purple corn, and a third full of what appeared to be a zucchini/carrot hybrid. It was a fact that no one went hungry on Lotus Lorea.

No mash turnip to be seen anywhere, though, thought

Cassidy. She felt an unexpected pang of homesickness.

This time Cassidy sat off to the side of the long table, trying to be as inconspicuous as possible, to fade into the background. It was something she was normally very adept at. This time, it didn't work. Everyone wanted to talk to the newcomer and all eyes were on her; everyone wanted her opinion on something. Finally, she gave up and joined in the conversation. It flowed around her like molten chocolate: warm, comforting and inviting. An embrace made entirely of words. Warmed by the soup and the repartee, Cassidy helped clean up and then, as another bell rang out signalling the end of day, she made her way back to her room.

And waited.

And waited some more, growing increasingly impatient.

An eerie silence descended on The Dorms as people settled in for the night. It occurred to her that perhaps it was only eerie to her, for she had less than noble intentions on her mind.

Cassidy lay on the bed, enveloped by the darkness, accompanied only by her thoughts and a jittery anticipation. What she wouldn't have given for an internet connection right now; a game of words with friends or a random Wikipedia article to pass the time, to distract her. She began to count off the minutes aloud, in a whisper. Cassidy waited a full hour. The time passed with excruciating slowness. Boots in her hand, she eased open the door, and listened. Silence. She tiptoed through the door in her stocking feet. No one in sight. It was go time.

She edged the door shut behind her and, keeping close

to the wall, she hurried down the steps and out the front door, taking much the same precautions as she had leaving the bedroom. The stillness outside was unlike anything Cassidy had ever experienced before. It felt as though she were the last person left in the world. The night air was sultry but not sticky; a light breeze lifted the hair off her shoulders. There was a marked absence of crickets and other creatures; no dogs barked; there were no late night revellers or couples out for a walk. The silence was absolute—save for the rush of her quickened breath.

She hauled her boots on and took off, stealthily, in the direction of the library.

***

Cassidy gave silent thanks for Marcella's passing remark that there were no locks anywhere. The library door swung open on well-oiled hinges and closed with a muffled *whoosh* behind her as Cassidy slipped inside. Orienting herself in the semi-pitch black, Cassidy left her boots near the circulation desk and tiptoed towards the stacks. She wasn't risking any noise at all, if she could help it.

The flashlight was exactly where she had left it, on the same shelf as the book she had come for; she didn't dare switch it on but it was an excellent marker. Earlier, she had tried to quickly memorize the order in which the books were placed on the shelf. She was sure that the third book to the right from where she had left the flashlight was *Letters Concerning the Gateway*. It was the one that interested her most. She had to make a quick choice and hoped that it was the right one. She edged the slim volume out from its space on the shelf and slipped it beneath the waistband at the back of her pants, tucking her shirt in around it so it fit securely. She pulled her jacket down as far as she could, hoping it would cover any visible bulk. She knew that it was imperative that she keep the book hidden. If she was unlucky enough to get busted out of The Dorms and walking around past curfew, she would simply lie about not being able to sleep and needing some fresh air. She hesitated for only a second before she slipped the tiny flashlight into her jacket pocket.

It never hurt to be prepared.

Mission accomplished. Her heart beating frantically despite the outward calm she displayed, she once again put her boots back on and, channelling her inner ninja, crept back towards The Dorms.

She had a little reading to do.

***

Adrenaline still pumping through her veins, Cassidy tumbled back into her room. She laughed breathlessly to herself and followed it up with a huge sigh of relief as she eased the door shut behind her. She'd met no one along the way—not that she'd expected to anyway, but her heart was pounding nonetheless, the sound of blood pumping in her ears. The rush was beyond compare.

She tossed the purloined flashlight and book onto the bed, slipped out of her coat and boots and climbed beneath the patchwork quilt. She made a platform with her knees, snapped on the flashlight and stifled a loud groan at what she saw in her hands: she'd stolen the wrong damn book. Of course she did. What she held in her hands was *Provenance and The Font*—of similar colour and size to *Letters Concerning the Gateway* but definitely *not* what she had risked sneaking out for. She swore elaborately and then finally sighed in resignation and accepted it for what it was. Perhaps all was not lost, she might learn something new after all. She definitely could not risk going out again. If she were caught this time, who knows what might happen. She had developed a repertoire with Marcella and she did not want to rock the boat. She was here for a reason; of that she was certain, even if that reason wasn't quite clear to her yet. It was not a good time to make enemies. And she was sure she would indeed make them if she was caught doing something untoward.

Opening the book, Cassidy directed the mediocre glow of the small flashlight toward the pages, and she began to read.

By the third page, Cassidy was more confused than anything else. The book was very, very old. It was handwritten and near impossible to decipher. There were a lot of what appeared to be formulas and incoherent ramblings scribbled along the margins. She could pick out a word here or there (*saved; spring; fountain*) but the faded ink and spidery cursive was sending her cross-eyed. She ran a hand through her already (perhaps permanently) dishevelled hair. All had been for naught. Disappointment swamped her. Hoping to at least salvage something from her nightly adventure, Cassidy flicked swiftly through the pages, careful to not damage them; scanning each page with a discerning eye lest a word might stand out to her as important.

It was a fruitless endeavour. She had learned nothing new and now she was in the possession of stolen property.

She grinned ruefully.

She had pulled a classic Cassidy.

CHAPTER SIX

She awoke bleary-eyed and disoriented, having fallen asleep mid-thought. It was a feeling she was used to, as she was so often beleaguered by jet lag. She waited until the fog cleared and the spinning stopped before she even considered moving from her prone position. She was sprawled across the rumpled bed; an uncomfortable lump digging into her ribs turned out to be the misappropriated flashlight. She remembered slipping the contraband book inside the pillowcase just before she'd finally succumbed to the exhaustion. The pillow, however, was somewhere on the floor. She groaned and rolled over, stretching sore muscles.

Abruptly, with a stunning clarity that sent her leaping from beneath the tangled sheets, she remembered the final words she'd been able to decode from the book before she'd passed out: *power* and *healing*.

She glanced down at her hand.

Eliza, please bring some water from the fountain to the infirmary. Marcella's voice came through clear and crisp in her mind, the memory bursting to the surface; her subconscious finally catching up.

She unwound her bandage and stared for a moment in stunned silence.

There was no mark on her hand at all. No indication that there had ever been an injury. No cut, no scab, no scar... just smooth, unblemished skin. She had seen the laceration across her palm. She had seen the blood. It would undoubtedly have required stitches. A scar would have been inevitable. Cassidy knew scars, she had many from her numerous adventures. She knew the drill.

This just was not possible.

Fuelled now by an insatiable need for answers, Cassidy dressed quickly, slipped from her room, and hurried down the stairs. She was fast but quiet, though she wasn't sure why—nearly everyone was in school or at work. Still, she crept past the shared living room area with its many shelves, heavy with books; the side tables stacked high with board games. There was knitting and cross stitch and any number of other crafts or hobbies one could choose to learn. Yes, she had been welcomed to Lotus Lorea with open arms and its residents had been nothing but cordial, warm and inviting—but a frisson of unease slithered down her spine. She glanced down at her hand once more and with a stubborn set to her shoulders, she slipped through the front door and stepped out into the sunlight.

Shielding her eyes against the glare, Cassidy tried to remember which route she needed to take that would bring her to the centre of town; was it left or right? Setting off at a steady, no nonsense pace, Cassidy's heavy boots scuffed louder than she would have liked. She sent furtive glances over her shoulder. Was Lotus Lorea the type of place to have surveillance? Probably not. But Cassidy was hardwired for paranoia.

She soon found herself in a small alleyway between two buildings. She had somehow taken a wrong turn. She closed her eyes and tried to centre herself. She had an excellent sense of direction normally but she felt jumbled and out of sorts; like her brain was waging a war between the Cassidy she was when she first arrived here and the Cassidy that was becoming inextricably linked to Lotus Lorea.

She began to retrace her steps.

Cassidy plunged back out of the opposite end of the narrow alleyway, her gaze fixed straight ahead, her focus entirely on the task at hand; she took no notice of the young girl observing her from the doorway of the library. With her earth-toned clothing she had blended in with the surroundings; Cassidy would never have known of her presence if not for the low bird-like whistle the girl gave; she inclined her head at Cassidy once she had gained her attention, and then, ever so slightly, pointed a finger to her left. Then she slipped back through the library door and out of sight. Quiet as a mouse.

That was… interesting to say the least. There had been something vaguely familiar about the girl, with the heart shaped face, the dark hair and the thick, impossibly long lashes. Cassidy filed the incident away at the back of her mind to mull over later when she had time to think it though, and then trotted off down the path that the girl had indicated. Within minutes, she emerged from the grass-lined trail and into the park that was adjacent to the town square. It was deserted, the only sounds those of the native birds that flittered from tree to tree, indulging in the sweet and sour berries produced by the domestic foliage. Their bright blue and ruby-red feathers stood out, easily visible against the green of the trees; their soft pitched calls to one another clear and pleasing to the ear. Like everything else here.

Trying to catch her breath, Cassidy bent at the waist, resting her hands on her knees. While she was down there her eyes roamed the grass, searching. She gave a small satisfied but short-winded grunt when she found what she was looking for. *Yes. That would work just nicely.* The rock was thin; not jagged but definitely sharp enough. She gritted her teeth and took a deep breath: no one could ever say she wasn't thorough in her research or committed to the cause. In one quick motion—before she could change her mind—she dragged the whetted edge of the rock across the palm of her left hand. She grimaced, her breath all at once hissing out through her front teeth at the sudden explosion of pain. White spots danced behind her eyelids. She closed her fingers over the quick deluge of blood that arose from the wound. Without hesitation, Cassidy sat on the edge, next to the stone child, and plunged her hand into the fountain. She spread her fingers wide and wiggled them around, watching as the whorls of crimson spread out across the surface of the water. The coolness of the water dulled the pain in her hand almost immediately. She glanced around to make sure she was still alone. How long should she wait? Her palm tingled. A pleasant warmth spread across her hand and out her fingertips. Heart pounding, Cassidy forced herself to remain still. She closed her eyes and silently counted to twenty, then forty, then sixty. Forcefully she made herself count as much again. Then, finally, unable to bear the suspense any longer, Cassidy withdrew her hand from the fountain and gazed in astonishment. Other than a small, thin red line, her hand had been mended. Within a day that line would most likely disappear and no one would ever know she'd been injured.

What the hell was she supposed to do now?

Wiping her still dripping hand on her trousers, Cassidy's mind whirled with the possibilities—though it was a cliché, those possibilities, right now, seemed quite endless. A fountain that …healed?! Gamgee would lose his mind over this.

Then it hit her. She laughed mirthlessly. *This* was why she was here.

He already knew.

Like the proverbial horse, she had been led to water.

CHAPTER SEVEN

The low-frequency siren whooped loudly through the town square, startling Cassidy as she sat, ruminating, on the same bench that she had sat on earlier with Marcella. She was so wound up from her shocking discovery, that the sudden barrage of sound made her jump and look around guiltily. Had she tripped some sort of alarm by touching the water in the fountain? Were they coming for her? Who would *they* even be? Her pulse raced.

"Don't be foolish," she muttered to herself. Her face coloured. She'd actually managed to embarrass herself with her ridiculous line of thinking. Maybe she had hit her head harder than she'd thought.

The rising cadence of the siren now sent people scrambling from everywhere; doors swung wide and Cassidy saw women running from all directions, some had not even paused to put on shoes. They all streaked past her and Cassidy, caught up in the urgency and the chaos, followed along.

Whoop, whoop, whoop.

Cassidy cringed. "What's going on?!" she shouted to the woman running next to her.

The woman gave her a strange look. "It's *a delivery*."

A delivery?

And then suddenly it all became clear. The medical centre loomed up ahead. Oh. It was *that* kind of delivery.

Cassidy rushed on forward, caught up in the crowd.

There was standing room only. People were huddled outside. In the main entryway a clique of teens was gathered together, chattering noisily and excitedly amongst themselves. An elderly lady shushed them, wagging a finger in their direction as she pushed past, into the lobby. Cassidy followed closely behind her, taking note of the teens' chagrined faces. There was the electric buzz of excitement in the air inside; hushed adult conversation was punctuated by barely stifled childish giggles and a rousing game of tag by the younger children that only added to the pandemonium. Cassidy made her way to the front of the throng, murmuring apologies, doling out smiles as necessary, as she excused herself past group after group of waiting women. They were all here to support each other. It was clearly a community event and it all seemed quite remarkable to Cassidy, this unique bond they all had—like something tied them together as one.

She spotted Marcella immediately, speaking to a tall bespectacled woman wearing a set of sparkling white scrubs. They both looked concerned, gesturing with their hands and frowning repeatedly.

"Is there anything I can do to help?" Cassidy interrupted. *This might be my way in.*

"Oh! Cassidy, hello! I didn't see you there."

"Is everything okay?"

"I'm afraid not, my dear. Well, nothing life threatening of course, just more of an inconvenience at the moment. This is Laura, she's our head midwife. She's been telling me that we are a little short-handed today."

"You don't have a doctor here?"

Marcella observed her curiously. "No, we have several trained midwives and a number of doulas."

A memory fired in Cassidy's synapses: *Hadn't Miss Ginny mentioned a doctor?*

Snapping out of it, Cassidy offered: "I have first aid training… if that's of any help?"

Marcella brightened. "Goodness yes! You are a lifesaver!" she gushed. "Just follow Laura to the back, that's where the birthing suites are."

Cassidy spared a glance over her shoulder and saw the looks of interest on the faces of those gathered in wait. Many were nodding and smiling in approval. She turned and followed Laura, leaving the whispers behind.

The deeper she went into the hospital, the more it became apparent that someone was in a great deal of pain. Cassidy did not have a great deal of experience in this sort of situation. In fact, what she knew of birth was in medical terms, from text books and, of course, from movies and television. The pain and screaming she had most definitely expected.

"Everlee is in active labour. We are getting quite close to the end now. I could definitely use a second pair of hands, just in case," Laura offered, smiling. "Now, you're not the queasy sort are you?"

Cassidy's eyes widened but she shook her head no and did not falter in step as she trailed along behind Laura. The screaming got louder. Cassidy winced. Together, the two women entered the small but clean and functional room that was, as Marcella had said, the birthing suite. Upon the bed at the centre of the room lay a young woman (Cassidy estimated her to be in her mid-twenties) drenched in sweat; tendrils of curly brown hair clung to her forehead and trailed into her eyes. She was breathing raggedly, bent forward over her knees as best she could, considering the large belly she was sporting in front. Holding her hand was the young girl Cassidy had encountered earlier. The same one who had shown her in which direction to find the fountain. Cassidy tried not to react.

"This is Everlee. Everlee, meet Cassidy. She's going to be giving me a hand since Lenora and Elsie are out with the flu. And Cassidy, this is Everlee's sister Ella."

Their eyes met briefly; an unspoken communication. "Nice to meet you, Ella."

"You too …Cassidy."

"Things will move quite swiftly now, Everlee," Laura said, stepping back from the bed where she had just administered a short examination.

Everlee grunted in reply, resumed her deep breathing and closed her eyes in concentration. Ella, stoic and glued to her sister's side, smoothed the damp hair back from her eyes and murmured what Cassidy assumed to be words of encouragement. Everlee quieted and nodded her head.

Laura guided Cassidy to the side of the room, showing her where to wash up and handing her a set of scrubs. "You can change into these in the room next door. It won't be long now so try to make it quick."

Everlee was already pushing, her face red and blotchy

with effort, when Cassidy returned to the room.

"Cassidy, are you ready?" Laura asked.

Cassidy took a deep breath, "As I'll ever be…"

***

The frantic high-pitched newborn wails filled the room and echoed off the walls. Cassidy stepped back in astonishment. She had never in all her days witnessed anything like this. She felt empowered and in complete awe of what Everlee had just accomplished. Everyone breathed a sigh of relief at the baby's cry—Everlee fell back against the pillows on the bed, her exhaustion apparent; Ella grabbed her hand and they smiled at each other. Both were crying.

"It's a boy," Laura announced quietly and Everlee gasped.

"No," breathed Ella. "Not again."

"Would you like to meet him before…?" Laura enquired.

Everlee turned away, her eyes full of unshed tears.

"Are you sure you don't want to? It is permitted. Many women choose to do so." Laura glanced at Ella as if looking for guidance but Ella shook her head curtly, and Everlee's only response was to curl onto her side and face the wall.

Cassidy, bewildered at the scene unfolding before her, watched as Laura wrapped the newborn in a soft blue blanket. She hummed under her breath and rocked him in her arms until he finally settled. Marcella appeared in the doorway, an eyebrow raised in question. Cassidy watched as she took in the scene, as she very quickly noticed the blue blanket. Her face fell. Laura walked to her and handed over the swaddled child.

"A boy," she said. Then, "Healthy. Strong lungs."

Marcella saw Cassidy looking at her and smiled softly, almost apologetically. "It is our way." And then she left with the baby as Everlee began to softly cry.

"This is bullshit!" Ella shouted as she ran from the room, knocking into Cassidy as she passed.

Laura shook her head, frowning. She seemed more upset at the language than the situation she'd just witnessed. She turned her attention back to Everlee, and Cassidy slipped unnoticed from the room. The medical centre had gone silent.

Everyone else had left.

The blue blanket—a signal.

Life would go back to normal now for everyone. For everyone, perhaps, but Everlee. And Ella. Cassidy was shaken. They'd taken the baby away. Just like that.

Cassidy heard muffled voices further down the hall; a door had been left ajar. She crept down the corridor, sidled up to the doorway, and strained to hear what was being said.

"Have they been chosen yet?"

"Yes, an older couple. They'd been waiting a long time before they found us. I've already made the call," came Marcella's voice.

"Wonderful! I'll leave with him shortly then."

"Yes, that sounds perfect! They'll take care of everything else back at The Agency. Out of necessity, this one will be heading out of state."

Footsteps approached; Marcella was leaving. Cassidy

looked around for a hiding spot and quickly slipped into a supply closet, coming face to face with mops, brooms, cleaning supplies, toilet paper, and the tear-stained face of Ella. Widening her red-rimmed eyes, her long dark lashes glistening with moisture, Ella quickly raised a finger to her lips, pursed them and emitted a small whisper of breath: *shhh*. Cassidy nodded once, a brief acknowledgement of her understanding and, with the greatest of care, she eased the door shut behind her.

She already had the answers to some of her questions.

She had a feeling she was about to find out a whole lot more.

CHAPTER EIGHT

A dim light came on overhead; a single bulb hanging on a thin string swung lazily to and fro, briefly illuminating their faces and then plunging them back into shadow. Cassidy averted her eyes and waited for Ella to compose herself. She didn't want to embarrass the girl anymore than she already was, having interrupted her in a private moment of loss and grief. Ella took deep shuddering breaths and swiped at her face with the sleeve of her tunic.

"Please. Don't tell them I'm in here!" Her high panicked tone raised Cassidy's hackles.

"It's cool. Don't worry. I won't say a word."

"Thank you," she replied with obvious relief, her shoulders visibly relaxing.

Cassidy eyed her curiously; she couldn't help but ask: "What happens if you're caught in here?"

"Caught spying? They'll send me to The Hut." She shuddered.

The Hut? Cassidy's thoughts drifted back to the small building she'd asked about while on the tour with Marcella. *The storage shed?*

"You don't want to know," Ella offered tremulously.

Oh, but Cassidy *did* want to know. She wanted to know very badly, but seeing the distress it was causing the girl, and along with everything else she had just had to deal with; Cassidy held her tongue, and her questions. Another time. Another place.

Ella gulped several deep breaths of air, swallowing her sobs.

In a faltering voice she whispered: "He's already gone isn't he?"

"Yes. I'm so sorry."

She sighed shakily but nodded her head, resigned. "It's for the best, I know that. But we still cared about him, you know? He'll be happy won't he? He'll go to a good home too, right?" she implored.

Cassidy wanted nothing more than to reassure the young woman. She knew that if all of the other parents chosen by The Rising Son Adoption Agency were anything at all like Annie and Ximena, the baby would have a wonderful home and would never want for anything. Cassidy knew that love was plentiful in the Romero-Jones house and Mateo would be cherished there.

"He will be loved. That's what they told me."

"He will," Cassidy answered; in her heart she felt it was the truth and she desperately wanted Ella to stop crying. She wasn't quite sure how to comfort her. And she didn't want to say the wrong thing. She was a bit out of her league with this whole entire situation; she just was not good with people and their emotions. Cassidy was accustomed to climbing mountains, tumbling out of cars, and breaking through windows; dodging bullets and belligerent aliens; exploring new worlds. Yet here, in this supply closet with this heartbroken girl—it was one of the scariest moments of Cassidy's life.

"Ella..." she began gently, questioningly.

Ella watched Cassidy intently, looking for signs of sincerity, clearly wanting to confide but also bound by what she had been taught her whole life was a secret. "It is our way."

"I've heard *that* before," Cassidy remarked dryly.

"It's better like this! Better than ways of old when…" She stopped, choked back another sob, unable to go on.

Cassidy was certain she understood what the *ways of old* might have entailed. She shivered. It was unimaginable.

The girl sniffed and wiped her nose on her arm again. Cassidy had been biting her tongue but curiosity had quickly overcome her.

"How often does this sort of thing happen, Ella? Baby boys being born here, I mean."

"Um…" she hesitated, her face darkening. "Not all that often. A few times a year maybe. Something goes wrong I guess. Usually when we… The fountain doesn't…" she trailed off. Her eyes widened, she flushed and an unreadable emotion flickered across her face.

"The fountain? What does the fountain have to do with this?" Cassidy jumped eagerly on what was clearly a slip up. She was eager for the big reveal.

Ella stared at Cassidy again for a few moments and Cassidy wondered if perhaps she'd spooked the girl, been a bit *too* eager. And then with a resigned look Ella began to speak, her voice taking on a reverent tone as she recited by rote: "At the time of the month, when the moon is high and the flower blooms, when we are of age and the time is right; when it is the path we have chosen to follow: we drink of the Lotus Fountain. It is our duty."

"But… what does that even…"

"It is our greatest blessing but also, sometimes, it is our greatest curse."

And then she slipped through the door, not making a sound, and was gone before Cassidy could say anything else. She didn't dare call out to her.

Cassidy sat abruptly on an upturned bucket—what the hell was going on in this place?! How did the fountain tie in with everything? And just what went on in that storage shed? Her mind whirled with all the snippets of information she'd gathered throughout the day, all the things she had learned about Lotus Lorea and the people who lived there.

Perhaps, after all, it was not nearly as perfect as it seemed.

Not one single bit.

She tiptoed to the door, opened it a crack, and waited until the coast was clear.

***

Walking back towards The Dorms, Cassidy gazed in wonder as the women around her carried on as though nothing remarkable had happened just a few short hours ago. As if a child had not been born. As if that child had not been whisked away …and then never spoken about again. Cassidy did not consider herself to be an overly maternal type but surely this wasn't normal behaviour, was it? No, not normal in her world, she realized, but perhaps this was nothing new here.

"Cassidy?"

The questioning voice broke her train of thought, star-tling her back to reality.

"I wanted to thank you for your assistance today. Lau-ra was very grateful, as I am sure Everlee was as well."

Marcella smiled at Cassidy as she turned around and faced her. Marcella took a step closer.

"I see something in you, Cassidy. You are a strong, intelligent woman, one who knows what she wants out of life; one who grabs it by the horns and doesn't let go. We need more people like you in Lotus Lorea. Someone our young girls can look up to ...like Ella does already." She paused. "This is rather unorthodox, and please, take all the time you need to consider my offer."

"Your offer?" Cassidy interrupted.

"Yes, my dear," Marcella continued. "Myself and the other elders have conferred and we would very much like it if you would stay on here. To join us permanently on Lotus Lorea."

At the look on Cassidy's face, a mixture of shock and bewilderment, Marcella quickly added: "Of course you could visit your own world as often as you like—the por-tal would remain open and at your disposal. But, your place, your *home*, would be here with us. There's a beau-tiful house just at the outskirts of the village. It could be yours. We are certain that, with a little bit of work, it could be turned into a lab or a research facility or whatever you want it to be! You would become an important part of our herstory."

"I... I don't..."

"Think about it, Cassidy, please. Take your time. Get

to know us, take your time and look around as much as you would like and then you can make your decision."

Marcella nodded at her, smiled a smile that seemed almost apologetic for having put her on the spot. She walked away in the direction of the town square, a slight droop to her shoulders.

Cassidy, still stunned at the proposition, made her way back to her room at The Dorms, lost once again in thought.

She felt disconcerted, perhaps even a little bit angry. Okay, she was a lot angry.

But mostly it was directed at herself.

Because, in the back of her mind, in the dark recesses that she kept hidden from everyone but herself, she was actually considering the offer.

***

She threw herself on the bed. She was being overly dramatic, she knew. Her mind flashed back to her teenage years when this very thing was a regular occurrence.

A long walk through the strawberry fields had helped to lessen her anger; the warm, fragrant breeze lifted the hair from her face and also helped to ease the tension from her shoulders. She'd stopped to watch some of the women as they prepped the soil for a new round of planting, and with some mild encouragement she found herself down on her knees, digging in the dirt and, to her surprise, thoroughly enjoying herself. Traces of soil still remained under her nails despite repeated scrubbings.

She had inspected The Hut as much as she dared, unable to resist the opportunity, being in such close proximity to it. Much to her disappointment, she wasn't able to get close enough to take a look inside one of its grubby windows. There was no way to bring up the topic without raising suspicion either, but the women were keen to keep a healthy distance from the building and that was something that did not escape her notice.

As the day wore on, she found herself invigorated by the work, and by the conversation and companionship of the women. She'd been invited to go around to Maggie's house for tea and a game of cards; Johanna insisted she come by and raid her closet, as Johanna was sure she had some things that would fit Cassidy perfectly. She glanced pointedly at Cassidy's now dirt smeared clothing and laughed. While they took a break in the shade of another weeping willow, sharing rich flaky scones slathered with a deep red berry jam, Cassidy enchanted them with stories of her own world. They seemed most interested in learning about cats and dogs, neither of which was native to Lotus Lorea.

"And you keep those things in your house? These animals with teeth and claws? Do people not fear it might gobble them up?!" asked a young girl named Ruth.

Cassidy laughed and then explained the deal with domesticated animals. They all listened intently with mouths agape, completely enthralled. Cassidy couldn't remember the last time she had been this relaxed; had spent this much time with people outside of work; had made friends. It was sobering. And invigorating. A different kind of adventure.

Here now, alone in her room once again, she stared at her dirty nails and everything rushed back to the forefront: the fountain, the birth; the adoption; Marcella's proposition, and the fact that she was actually thinking about staying. What was she thinking?!

She recalled all the occasions where, despite her level of education and her expertise in the field of Archaeology, and despite years of hard work and countless accolades for her accomplishments, she was still no where near on the same scale as her male counterparts. She was, of course, successful in her own right, this was true, but she could still imagine how it would feel to be at the top in her profession and *not* be ridiculed for her ideas simply because she was a woman. She read the hateful comments online even though she knew she shouldn't. She overheard the not-so-whispered remarks behind her back at conferences and the *can you believe this chick?* chuckles from the male dominated audiences as she gave keynote speeches. She shook her head, no, she would not be sad to leave *that* behind, of that she was certain.

She could have everything she had always wanted.

Here on Lotus Lorea.

But that was the catch.

Could she leave her old life behind?

Tangled up with all this disillusionment about what she should do were also her heavy suspicions that Gamgee was more than aware of the portal she had used to get here, that he'd known what was on the other side and that he'd had his own motives for encouraging her to investigate the mystery of the adoption agency when she'd brought it up to him. She could not understand all this subterfuge, these games, when it had never been necessary before.

Then again… there was The Lotus Fountain to consider. It was quite remarkable, was it not? And that meant that there was a lot more at stake this time around. It also meant greater consequences. The burden of those consequences would now fall to Cassidy, and Cassidy alone.

She once again considered the possibilities and was wracked with indecision. Didn't she owe it to her world to bring back, at the very least, a sample of the water from the fountain? Gamgee… he could reproduce it. It would change everything, save countless lives.

But if she did that, well, surely she would have to destroy the portal. There would be war between the worlds otherwise. But then, The Rising Son Adoption Agency would be no more once the portal no longer existed. Cassidy would cut off their connection. What right did she have to do so? Surely they would then revert back to their *ways of old*. Cassidy couldn't bear the thought.

She arose from the bed and paced around and around the small room, chewing on her thumbnail, furiously cursing under her breath as she did so. See, that was the problem: she had too much time to think. Yes, that's definitely what it was. She was a woman of action and all this inaction was the foundation of her problems. She prided herself on *not* thinking—which, she was fully aware, sounded like quite a bizarre mantra, but she was a person who just went for it, consequences be damned.

Maybe it was time to take that leap.

Just go for it.

And that was when the knock sounded at the door.

CHAPTER NINE

"I'm afraid we have a bit of a problem."

Cassidy opened the door wide to allow Marcella to enter. The normally composed matriarch rung her hands. She was very visibly upset; there were beads of sweat gathered on her temples and her hair was in disarray. She looked at Cassidy imploringly; having stated that there was a problem she now appeared lost for words, or maybe even afraid to speak them.

"What's wrong?!" Cassidy exclaimed.

She bit her lip, then squared her shoulders before she began: "We cannot find Ella or Everlee. Laura has told me that Everlee left the clinic not long after the birth. No, it is not unheard of for women to check out early if they have family at home who can care for them but… we think they may have…" She swallowed with difficulty, struggled to get the words out. She finally met Cassidy's eyes and took a deep breath. "We think they may have accessed the portal." Then, all in a rush: "It is *strictly* forbidden."

"Don't you have a guard or something posted to it?!"

"No. There has never been a need. No one leaves. It is paradise. Why would they ever want to?"

Looks like someone did, Cassidy thought ingeniously.

"What do you need me to do?"

"Thank you, Cassidy! I knew you would help." Marcella sighed in relief and managed a flicker of a smile. "Would you go after them? They are not prepared for your world. It is so unlike ours. I am very worried for their safety! And who better to navigate it than you?"

Marcella had every right to be worried. Those two girls, ingénue as they were, would be sitting ducks, especially if they ventured outside the gated community of Carina Heights. And maybe even *inside* the gates if they ran into the wrong people.

"How much of a head start do you think they had?"

"We can't be sure. An hour, perhaps longer, but not much more than that."

"I'll go."

Marcella's appreciation was evident. "I knew you would help. Please… bring them home."

***

Cassidy rushed into her room at The Dorms and quickly gather up what little possessions she had with her. She jammed her useless cell phone in a back pocket, crammed the random bits she'd carried with her—lip balm, keys, a few dollars in coins, a roll of breath mints—back into another pocket. There was an urgency to her movements and she was back out on the street within minutes. A small group had gathered: Marcella, Laura and a few other faces Cassidy recognized from those she'd encountered, the friends she had made. Johanna, Maggie and Ruth.

They looked at her expectantly.

"I'll find them."

She nodded resolutely, meaning every word she had said, and took off at a run, heading along what was now a familiar route. The portal was midway up a cliff side on the south border of the village, a short distance from The Lotus Fountain. A set of stone stairs had been roughly hewn into the face of the rock—stairs that Cassidy had tumbled down unceremoniously when she had first arrived in this world—but had, over the years, from weather and use eroded into smooth, uneven edges. It hadn't been that long ago, but it felt like forever. She ascended the steps without hesitation, feeling the familiar thrum, that pulsing along her veins, the closer she got to the portal. She was high on the thrill of the chase; gone was the calmness and serenity she'd achieved during her brief stay on Lotus Lorea.

She felt useful.

Alive.

It was glorious.

Cassidy burst through the portal; the baby-fine hairs on the back of her neck and along her forearms quivered and stood at attention as the brief zap of energy flowed through her in a rush. It was not an unpleasant feeling. More so, it was something Cassidy associated with action, adventure and, yes, a whole hell of a lot of fun.

Unfortunately, fun was the one thing she was not having right now, even if on some level she was enjoying the thrill of the chase, the sense of purpose.

Her unexpected appearance in a back room of the adoption agency, which had now opened for business, startled those who had already started their workday, their office doors open wide and ready for clients who would soon arrive. There they sat in front of their computers, mouths agape in shock as Cassidy, who had seemingly appeared out of nowhere, strolled past. The existence of the portal was definitely on a need-to-know only basis in this place and these folks definitely did *not* know.

A cluster of minions had gathered near the water cooler, shooting the breeze. Ignoring the file folders in their hands, they seemed quite relaxed and utterly unaware of the hellfire that was about to rain down on them.

Cassidy—the aforementioned hellfire—fists clenched by her side, face flushed with suppressed emotions, shouted: "Two girls! Have two young girls gone through here?"

One woman squeaked in fright and dropped the folder she'd been holding. Another sloshed a small paper cup of water down the front of his suit and tie as he reacted to the squeak.

"Where in the world did you come from?!" The startled exclamation came from a ginger bearded man sporting thick black rimmed glasses and holding a clip board. "There isn't supposed to be anyone back here but employees of the agency!"

Cassidy rolled her eyes. "Listen, pal, I don't have time for your crap right now. I'm looking for two girls. Young, most likely scared. Have you seen them in this building or anywhere near here?"

"We haven't seen anything," he replied indignantly.

"How long have you all been here?!" Cassidy questioned, eyes narrowed.

"Ten... maybe fifteen minutes," sputtered the squeaker and dropper of file folders. "We haven't seen anyone other than our coworkers, I swear. And, well, now you too." She faltered, bit her lip nervously and looked away from Cassidy's penetrating gaze.

She seemed scared, Cassidy suddenly realized, like she expected Cassidy to haul out a weapon and start shooting. Cassidy had the grace to feel chagrined for her aggressive behaviour, but the moment, and the thought, was fleeting.

"Dammit all."

Cassidy ran past them all, ignoring their confusion and their rapidly burgeoning curiosity. They flattened against the walls, allowing her quick, unfettered passage down the hall. One man reached out as if to stop her but then reconsidered, his hand left dangling there in mid-air as Cassidy shot him a dark cautionary look over her shoulder, warning him in no uncertain terms, hands off.

Unlike the night before, when she had had to be clandestine and sneaky, when she had creeped in through a back window like a thief under cloak of darkness, Cassidy blew past the reception desk and out through the front door as bold as brass, exploding out into the stark bright light of day, her mind on one thing: the mission to bring Everlee and Ella back to their home. It would be a bittersweet endeavour.

It smelled different here. And not in a good way. That was her first coherent thought of her own home as she hit the ground running. It wasn't that she had really been gone all that long but her senses had already adjusted to the absence of exhaust fumes, heavy perfume, cleaning chemicals and other offensive scents that were not native to Lotus Lorea.

She chose to ignore a pang of something that felt re-markably like home sickness.

She was missing something she had never really had to being with.

So, where to now?

Directly across the road from where she stood, an older woman in a voluminous purple coat was walking a ridiculously small dog along the sidewalk. Cassidy trot-ted down the curved driveway at the front of The Rising Son Adoption Agency, waved at the pedestrian and then, when that failed to catch her attention, she shouted: "Hey! Excuse me! Ma'am?! Can I speak to you for a moment?"

The woman stopped and regarded Cassidy with sus-picion. Cassidy didn't blame her. The lady's tiny furred companion sent up a raucous yapping at her approach, spinning in circles, tangling both itself and its owner in the short bejeweled leash attached to a gem encrusted col-lar. Cassidy imagined how intrigued her new friends on Lotus Lorea would be by this chipper creature.

"Hush, Kevin!!"

Kevin?

Cassidy raised her voice over the enthusiastic bark-ing that showed no signs of slowing down. "Have you seen two young girls anywhere near here? One has long, straight black hair, the other is a curly brunette. Very pret-ty. Maybe 5'3" or thereabouts? One may need immediate medical attention."

"I'm sorry, no, I haven't seen anyone other than a few other dog walkers and a couple of joggers. But I see those people nearly every day when me and Kevsie get out for a trot. Don't we, Kevin?! You like going walksies don't you, my good boy?!"

The lady continued to speak in a chirpy, singsong voice to the dog. Cassidy raised an eyebrow and backed away quickly, muttering a thank you under her breath as she made her escape. The woman didn't seem to notice. She was fully absorbed with Kevin.

Cassidy scanned the area. Where would they go? *Come on, Cassidy, think!* She hauled her damaged phone out of her pocket and powered it up.

"Please, please," she murmured, mentally crossing her fingers, hoping against hope that it would work, and that there was enough charge left for what she had in mind.

Victory. The easily recognizable logo popped below the shattered screen as the phone gloriously glowed to life. Battery at 13%. That would have to do. She scrolled through her contacts and crossed her fingers that this one phone call wouldn't completely deplete what was left of her battery.

"Hello there, Cass—"

"Are there any vacant houses in Carina Heights?" Cassidy broke in, her abruptness not completely out of character.

"Well, good morning to you too, Ms. Cane. Planning a move are we?" came the immediate response.

Cassidy was not in the mood for a witty repartee. She took a deep breath. Gamgee would be dying of curiosity; Cassidy was absolutely sure of it—especially if her suspicions were on the money. She wasn't giving up anything right now. Let him think she had not fallen for the bait.

She forced a laugh. "Not anytime soon. Just out for

some fresh air and a bit of exploring, you might say."

"I see. Well, it's not the best neighbourhood, I'm afraid. At one time it was very family oriented. There is an old cul-de-sac, I believe; development was eventually abandoned on it. It's on the Southside. Frecker. No! Fraser Place, that's it. Perhaps that would suit your needs?"

Perhaps it would indeed.

"Great! Thanks so much, Doctor! Bye for now."

"Will I see you at the university later?"

Cassidy paused; shook her head to herself. There was no time for this idle chat. "Sorry, my phone is about to die!" The words came out in a rush and Cassidy very quickly ended the call before Gamgee could interject again.

She accessed the maps application on the phone, tapped in Fraser Place and quickly memorized the route she would need to take to get to the subdivision.

Nine percent.

She shoved the phone with its worrisome low battery percentage back into her pocket and took off at a run through the park. If she was right, it would be a shortcut and her destination time would be cut nearly in half.

Cassidy was a fast runner. A skill born of necessity and well cultivated over the years from dodging bullets and escaping bad tempered nasties—both of the alien *and* human kind.

It was much better than a gym workout.

She vaulted a bench, not just because it was in her way but simply because it was there and she could. She grinned, pleased that she was still agile enough to do such things. Blood pumping, now that the adrenaline had kicked in, coursing through her veins. Sweat beaded on her forehead

and the back of her neck; parched, she longed for a cold
bottle of water. Her breath rushed in and out of her mouth
and she felt the hit in her calves as the lactic acid she was
producing flooded her muscles. The slapping of her feet
on the ground matched the hammering of her heart and
as she exited the tree line that encircled the park, Cassidy
finally hit her stride, that runner's high that everyone talk-
ed about. Her body pumping like a well oiled machine
now, Cassidy began to calculate all of the likely scenarios
she might possibly face when she reached her final destination. Everlee had only just given birth. There could be
any number of complications and she could require immediate medical attention. Not to mention the repercus-
sions for the both of them from having gone through the
portal. Even Cassidy, after her many travels, still felt the
jolt to her very core as she passed through the doorways
between worlds. Cassidy hoped there would be enough
charge left on her phone to call 911 if it was necessary.
She would worry later about the consequences of two un-
documented females, without medical cards, insurance or
any sort of ID. She'd figure something out. She was good
at flying by the seat of her pants.

As she mulled over the situation, she wondered how
the girls had managed to make it past the guards at the
agency; how they had been able to make it as far as they'd
gotten, given their lack of experience outside their own
world. It took some planning, ingenuity and cunning.
Cassidy suspected that Ella might have spearheaded the
whole escape.

Inside, Cassidy was secretly impressed.

She hit Fraser Place at a dead run; the cul-de-sac was

larger than she expected but was still spread out before her as she had expected, its typical semi-circle shape coming to an abrupt end where construction had ceased on new houses. She slowed to a jog. Carina Heights had, at one time, clearly expected to grow by leaps and bounds. She stood facing several fully built houses, a few on each side of the street, with for sale signs still pegged into their front lawns, though most now sagged at a jaunty angle. At the very end of the road, foundations had been laid down for at least five more structures. Those basement spaces were now overgrown with weeds, filled with garbage and whatever else had blown or rolled in. Heavy equipment sat dormant, deserted and rusted on the gravel driveways and atop bare patches of dirt that, had the neighbourhood come to fruition, been covered in lush green lawns. All was quiet save for the soft rustle of the breeze through the trees and the occasional whistle of a bird. Cassidy was far enough away now that even Kevin's sharp yaps were no longer audible.

She surveyed the houses, wheels churning in her head. Ella was a clever girl; she'd pick a hiding place that would be safe for her and her sister. Which house would she choose? Cassidy bit her lip. Then it clicked. Ella would want electricity if possible, running water, a working toilet—amenities Everlee would need as she recovered from the birth. Angling her head skywards, Cassidy eyed the power lines running from the poles; she followed their serpentine trails straight from the pole to the one and only house where they had been connected, and where, presumably, electricity still flowed. Number 1 Fraser Place.

"That's it," she whispered to herself.

Cassidy made a beeline for the front door. She saw no sense now in playing coy. There was no need to knock. Instead she simply twisted the handle. It was locked. Because of course it was. She took a step back and squinted in the glaring sun, glancing upwards at the second floor windows. A curtain twitched.

Cassidy smiled.

Gotcha.

CHAPTER TEN

"Have they been located?"

"Yes, ma'am. They'd gone for a walk along the south fields and stayed there, near the water, for a while to rest and eat."

"I expected as much. Thank you."

"And, what of the visitor?"

"It's been... taken care of."

***

The top step creaked as Cassidy leaned forward to peer through the grubby window. Cupping her hands around her eyes, she squinted in the low light that extended beyond the door. No movement. No sign that anyone at all was staying there, as a matter of fact; no stray shoes scattered across the floor or a jacket abandoned over the back of a chair, no backpack or purse... nothing like the permanent "lived in" look that was the constant esthetic at Cassidy's house. Ella, or Everlee, or whoever it was who had peeked through the curtain in the upstairs room, already knew that she was there, but still Cassidy shrugged and raised a hand to knock firmly on the door.

"Everlee? Ella? It's me, Cassidy!" Impatiently she

waited; was met with silence. She knocked again, sharply. Concern furrowed her brow.

"It's okay, I promise! I'm just here to help! You can let me in!" she shouted, hoping she had been loud enough to be heard inside.

Another flicker at the window upstairs. The blue floral curtains swayed ever so slightly, as though having just been kissed by a light summer draft. There *was* someone there—she had not just imagined it.

Concern was quickly giving way to suspicion now. There was absolutely no reason for Everlee or Ella to be afraid of her. Why would they continue to hide and ignore her calls?

Cassidy took a step back. And then another. A frisson of awareness trailed its frigid fingers down her spine. A dog howled shrilly in the distance.

Something wasn't right.

Her gut instinct was telling her to run, to run now and not stop—and she trusted her gut implicitly. She'd gotten no further than fifty feet up the road when the explosion ripped through the house, sending flames shooting high into the sky and echoing with horrifying certainty throughout the gated community of Carina Heights. The colossal blast hit Cassidy in the back, a blazing hot smack that lifted her unapologetically off the ground and tossed her like a ragdoll. She tumbled through the air, an agonizing slow motion freefall that ended abruptly as she smashed into the ground, the landing leaving her winded on the grass of a house all the way on the other side of the road.

Flaming debris, glass, and metal shrapnel showered

around her and she instinctively covered her head and face with her arms as she tried to catch her breath. Chunks of scorched wood thumped onto the ground around her and she counted her lucky stars that none of them had hit her. When the worst of the explosion and the fallout seemed to have passed she did a quick army crawl to the safety of the houses covered porch.

What in the actual hell had just happened here?

Breath coming in wracking gasps that bordered on hyperventilation, Cassidy dragged herself up the steps and collapsed against the emerald green door of number 7. She winced in agony at the high pitched whine that was a constant ringing in her ears, and the pain at the base of her skull that throbbed in time to the beat of her heart. She assessed her injuries, of which there were many, and grimaced: the hand that came away from her scalp was slick with her own blood. Her eyes streamed; she wasn't sure if they were tears of pain or from the thick smoke that stung them.

For a brief moment, Cassidy thought of the healing powers of The Lotus Fountain and found herself giggling hysterically.

Then she slumped to the ground, bleeding and unconscious.

***

The wailing of sirens roused Cassidy to awareness. She groaned loudly as she pushed herself back into a sitting position. How long had she been out for? The smouldering ruins of the house on the cul-de-sac still sent dark whorls of smoke spiralling into the cloudless cerulean skies above Carina Heights, turning them murky and ashen. Small areas of fire still burned; hungry for fuel, fingers of flame reached out for the woods beyond what once had been someone's home.

A home that had just been completely obliterated.

Her head was spinning, but if Cassidy knew one thing, it was that she did not want to be here when the emergency responders arrived. They would have a lot of questions and the one thing she did not have was answers. She gingerly assessed the wound at the back of her head and deemed it to be not life threatening. Rising slowly to her feet, she fought back brutal waves of nausea and dizziness. She took deep shaking breaths and focused on the act of standing and remaining upright. The acrid smoke from the explosion and continuing blaze wafted in her direction; she coughed and gagged, retching on the scent, vomiting over the side of the front steps into the hydrangea bushes. Well, at least that was out of the way. Swiping a hand across her mouth, Cassidy stumbled down the steps, reoriented herself, and set off at a slow agonizing jog, putting distance between herself and Fraser Place. She ducked under the cover of trees in the park that occupied the centre of Carina Heights; she paused beside an American elm, leaning against its trunk to catch her breath, her hands and knees shaking—a delayed reaction to the shock of what had just happened. Still beneath the leaves, she watched as a long string of emergency vehicles flew past where she stood and on up into the cul-de-sac, sirens screeching and lights flashing red and white. The shockwaves of the explosion had no doubt been felt for miles around.

If there had been anyone in that house… Cassidy didn't even want to think about it.

Couldn't think about it.

She turned her back on the scene, pushing it from her mind and plodding on forward, as she always did. She took stock of her ripped and stained clothing. The heavy scent of smoke clung to her hair and skin; her hands were bloodstained, her nails filthy.

She was a sorry sight.

And the person who orchestrated this whole thing too, once she got her hands on them, oh yes, they would be a sorry sight as well.

Cassidy burned with the need for revenge. Someone would pay for this. And she had a pretty damn good idea who that person would be.

***

Cassidy walked in through the door of The Rising Son Adoption Agency just like she owned the place. She heard the gasps of shock from the young woman on the front reception desk, saw her push back her chair to rise, but Cassidy did not pause in her stride. She chortled to herself, imagining what the poor woman must be thinking at the sight of her, like an extra from *The Walking Dead*. Cassidy continued beyond the outer foyer and towards the inner offices and then, down that now familiar hall. She had no trouble finding it now, and as people poked their heads out of various office doors she tipped an imaginary hat at them, smirking as they quickly ducked back inside and shut their doors. A lot of people felt that way about Cassidy even when she *wasn't* covered in soot and blood. She was surprised no one had called the cops on her yet.

Cassidy punched in the security code on the pad with only the briefest of glances. She threw open the door to the room holding the portal and slipped inside. The door swung shut behind her, the lock mechanism clicking securely. She wouldn't be bothered this time. She headed straight through the portal without pause, the zap of energy running through her; it was much needed energy that would fuel her for what was ahead. It was time for some answers—she would demand those answers, dammit—and she was going to be the one asking all the questions.

This time when she arrived there was much less fanfare, but she wasn't in much better shape. To Cassidy, blood and Lotus Lorea seemed to go hand in hand. She quickly and deftly descended the stone steps and planted her feet on the now familiar cobbled pathways of the world of Lotus Lorea.

There wasn't a soul in sight.

She would take a direct approach, for there was no need for subtleties. In all honesty, Cassidy could not have been bothered. She was too tired to be subtle. The time, the energy—she was far beyond that right now. In spite of all their insistence that they were the embodiment of tranquillity and peace, Lotus Lorea was not nearly as perfect as they wanted everyone, and especially Cassidy, to believe. She set off at a steady pace along the path that would take her to the centre of town. There would be no healing waters for her this time around, no mending of clothes, no welcoming party or lavish meals. If her suspicions were correct, the Lotus Loreans were more about hurting than healing.

As she began to near the centre of town, as she strode past the housing units and along the main thoroughfare, Cassidy began to come across more and more people. They filed out of doorways as if they sensed that something big was about to happen. They huddled together in small groups, whispering; their faces aghast at the sight of her and, perhaps, even a little fearful. She did not blame them one bit. They had a right to be afraid. And she was willing to take each and every one of them on if she had to. Not only had they messed with her—and very nearly gotten her killed!—but they had also messed with someone she cared about.

Cassidy saw Marcella, had a moment to assess her, before the matriarch saw her. She was chatting animatedly with another woman, laughing and smiling as though she had not one care in the world. That was about to change.

How dare she?! What kind of monster is she?! wondered Cassidy.

"Did you try to blow me up?! What about Ella and Everlee?! Do you realize what you have done?!" Cassidy demanded, her voice dripping with malice and rising higher and higher in octave, raging with each and every word, until the final one came out as a scream, the cords in her neck straining with the force of her emotion.

Marcella recoiled as though she had been physically struck. Her reaction from the shock of seeing Cassidy in front of her and the onslaught and venom of Cassidy's words—they were like a slap in the face. "I… I don't know what you are talking about!" she stammered, feigning innocence.

"Like hell you don't!" Cassidy sneered, spitting out each syllable as through it had left a bad taste in her mouth.

A small crowd had begun to gather in the square behind Cassidy. They all watched with a keen interest and there was a sizzle of anticipation in the atmosphere.

How long before someone showed up with the popcorn?

Marcella had backed up against the fountain, her hand upon her chest—Cassidy thought for sure that if Marcella had been wearing a string of pearls around her lying neck, she would have been clutching them, meme style. In spite of the seriousness of the situation, Cassidy felt a giggle bubble in her chest. Maybe she *had* acquired a head injury in the blast.

Cassidy licked her lips, ready for a war of words; her weapon of choice. She took one step closer. It was war she was sure she could win. "Why the hell did you try to kill me?!"

Marcella began to shake her head in denial. Her eyes moved frantically, searching for an ally or a way out; she was like a rat trapped in a corner and Cassidy was the hungry cat, claws out. Marcella murmured 'no' over and over again, repeatedly, under her breath.

"Hey!" Cassidy shouted, moving forward to snap her fingers right under Marcella's nose. Marcella's eyes popped open and the tears began to tumble down her face.

Marcella stammered; the words inaudible, barely above a whisper. She was a shell of the woman Cassidy had met when she first arrived. Absolutely pathetic.

"Speak up!!" Cassidy demanded, disgusted. The growing crowd behind them leaned forward nearly in unison and held their breath in anticipation. They appeared to be just as invested in these answers as Cassidy was.

Marcella began to sob inconsolably as, bit by bit, her voice wavering and cracking, the story tumbled out.

"They were only supposed to scare you! That's all! Just scare you! Not hurt you, I swear. I never wanted that. My goddess almighty, they were never ever supposed to try and kill you! What did they do?!"

"They?" Cassidy breathed menacingly.

"I… I can't… No."

"Oh you can, and you bloody well will."

Marcella once again dissolved into tears. "Cassidy, I cannot apologize enough to you… "

"You can take your apologies and jam them up your…" Cassidy took a deep breath. "Who are *they*?" she repeated.

Marcella clammed up and shook her head.

Miss Ginny stepped forward from a throng of people standing outside the library. Cassidy hadn't even noticed her there; she was so blind with rage she might not have noticed anyone.

"Marcella! What is going on here?!"

Marcella glanced at Miss Ginny, their gaze met. Marcella took a deep shuddering breath and finally nodded her head. Out of nowhere someone handed her a handkerchief. She blew her nose loudly. Her red-rimmed eyes met Cassidy's fiery expression. Finally, beaten at a game she should never have tried to play, she spoke.

"They were only supposed to scare you. The security

team that was hired to protect the agency, to keep strangers away, to discourage snooping from the people who work there. They were *never* meant to harm you!"

"And what about Everlee and Ella? Were *they* supposed to just *scare* them as well?! *They* blew up a house!"

"No! No! They were never missing to begin with!"

Cassidy flinched in shock. "What did you say?!"

"It was all a ruse. A lie to get you to leave. It was the only way I could think of to get you away from here. I am so sorry."

"Where are they? Have you put them in your Hut?" Cassidy spat, making no attempt to hide her disgust.

"No! I swear, they are safe. And no, before you ask, they were not in on this deception at all. Ella would never have consented to that. She has taken a very real liking to you," Marcella finished sadly, lowering her head, her voice thick with suppressed tears and emotion; she was defeated.

Cassidy ran her grubby hands through her hair. It was a tangled mess, sticky with half congealed blood at the back. She probably needed stitches. She would worry about that later... once this place was in her rear view mirror.

"Why?" The question came out softly. There was no malice now, just a need to know. Cassidy was tired. So very, very tired. The fight had gone out of her now that she knew that Ella and Everlee were safe.

Marcella sniffled. "You would *not* have stayed, I could see that—and we really did want you to! But we knew what would have happened once you left here. In all good conscience I could *not* let you do that to us. We needed to scare you away somehow. Sacrifices had to be made for the greater good."

The portal. Marcella knew that if Cassidy had decided not to stay, if she had left Lotus Lorea for good, the portal would have had to be destroyed. Somehow, she knew the drill.

Cassidy felt a burning sense of betrayal; a twinge of humiliation and the paralysing rush of guilt. Because that is exactly what would have happened.

As she felt her legs crumple beneath her, her last coherent thoughts were disappointment commingled with sadness for all that could have been and all that would never be.

CHAPTER ELEVEN

A cup of strong, sweet *jaroot* with what appeared to be quite a liberal dash of rice milk sat waiting for Cassidy on the small table in her room. Beside that, on a tray, a thick slice of almond cake similar to Norwegian Kransekake; generous morsels of sharp goat's milk cheddar, and a bowl of large luscious blueberries lightly drizzled with lavender honey.

Cassidy wanted to partake of the lavish spread before her but her heart just wasn't in it; neither was her stomach. It was almost as though she felt nothing at all, a weird muted non-feeling that was entirely unique to anything she had ever experienced before.

She had returned after a short walk and had been left here alone simply because she had asked to be, really *had* wanted to be alone, but when a knock came to the door presently, she sprung quickly to her feet, eager to see what she hoped would be a friendly face. She cringed at the insistent pain at the back of her head, the wound having not quite healed, and the agonizing twinge of her still stiff and sore muscles, her aching joints.

"Come in!"

A head peeked around the door. It was Ella. Of course it was.

"Hello," she offered tentatively, flashing a shy grin.

"Hello."

Ella's concerned gaze brushed over the untouched food, Cassidy's defeated demeanour. She quickly took stock of the myriad of cuts, bruises and abrasions on every visible inch of Cassidy—her imagination filled in the injuries she could not see. Ella shook her head at the stubbornness of her new friend.

"You should at least drink your *jaroot* today, Cassidy. I made it myself, especially for you. I think you will feel a whole lot better afterwards." She smiled teasingly, winked, and backed out of the room. "I'll check on you in the morning. Bright and early as usual okay?"

Cassidy nodded. And after the door was closed behind Ella, Cassidy finally gave in and drank the *jaroot*.

Then she ate the cake and the cheese and the berries—devoured it with relish. Belly full, she returned to the bed, lying back on the feather down pillow, luxuriating in the relief as the stiffness seeped from her weary, bruised and battered body; there really was no greater feeling than the cessation of pain.

In repose, her mind wandered and ruminated over her exploits of the last little while. And the final confrontation with Marcella.

Cassidy had not returned to her room at The Doors. Once she had recovered well enough to leave the infirmary she had been made welcome at the home of Ella and Everlee. She was comfortable there as she recuperated, having been kept company by their elderly grandmother

Diana and a younger cousin, Melody.

Marcella, her lesson learned, had stepped down from her tutelary role. A decision would be made later, once the community came to terms with what had happened, on who would take her place. Her last instruction had been to order a decommissioning of The Hut, a place of punishment that had been largely kept secret from the population of Lotus Lorea, save for those who had been disciplined by being locked inside.

At least some good had come out of it all.

Everlee, who had since recovered from the birth (something she still refused to speak of) had applied to the vocational school, hoping to be educated in the field of midwifery. She wanted a better experience for the other women who gave birth on Lotus Lorea. That was something that would never change. It was an integral part of who they were.

Ella found herself thinking that she might eventually train to become a nurse. Between caring for her grandmother, Everlee, *and* Cassidy, she had learned it was something she enjoyed and had a flair for—helping people, making them well again. The book that Cassidy had been reading in the library on tinctures, poultices and herbal remedies had been checked out so many times that Miss Ginny finally told Ella she could just keep it.

Miss Ginny. She was a mystery, that one. And Cassidy supposed that some mysteries were better left unsolved. Cassidy had some ideas, naturally, but decided to keep the conjecture to herself.

Cassidy flashed back to the day she'd stumbled upon the secret of The Lotus Fountain. How it was such a strange coincident that Ella had happened to be in the right place, at the right time, right there outside the library, directing Cassidy along the right path. Suddenly, something finally clicked in her head, two and two came together at last in an explosive revelation and Cassidy's eyes popped open with a start. Ella. The dark hair. The heart shaped face. Those impossible lashes. A wave of sadness rocked her to her core. *Oh dear god no. That poor girl.*

Then, as the *jaroot* worked its magic, a pleasant drowsiness overcame her and, though she fought it, she finally succumbed to the oblivion of sleep.

***

She left while everyone else was still in bed. She was not the sort of person who was very good with goodbyes and she did not want to delay the inevitable now that she had made her final decision. A note for Ella was left behind, on the bed next to the pillow where Cassidy was sure that her friend would find it when she came looking for her in early hours of morning. It was so much better, much easier this way. For everyone involved. Cassidy felt the vestiges of regret but pushed them deep down inside as she snuck out of the house and into the silken embrace of night.

Dear Ella,

You are such a strong person. Thank you for everything; for taking care of me while I recuperated, but most of all, I want to thank you for being a friend. I know now that despite everything, I belong in my own world and it is time for me to go back there now. Come to the stone steps at the base of the cliff. Come alone. There will be something waiting there for you. Keep it to yourself. It is the only way I can think to repay you.

    C.

A sullen moon gave very little in the way of light as Cassidy's battered boots scuffed along the cobbled stone path that would lead her to the cliff side and, eventually, to the portal. She would go back to her own world with its trials and tribulations and perfect imperfections because, even with all its faults, it was still *home*.

The building that occupied The Rising Son Adoption Agency was dark and quiet save for the drone of machines and the light of computer screens left running with their screensavers dipping and swirling, as Cassidy arrived back Earth side. It was evening here—the fluidity of time, the flip flop of day and night between here and there threw her off balance every single time, her body and mind struggling to adjust to the fluctuations. She punched in the lock code and when the mechanism clicked, she exited the room, her shoulders set, a sense of purpose to her step. The door swung shut behind her. She strolled down the hallway and made her way to the office she had entered on that very first night.

The door was locked.

"Goddammit all!" she muttered under her breath.

There was no keypad with which she could gain entry but Cassidy was as determined as she ever had been. She refused to let a flimsy little lock like that stop her. She put everything she had left into it, all the pent up anger and emotion, and with one swift, well aimed kick near the doorknob, the wood panel door splintered and Cassidy shouldered her way in through, booting detritus and debris out of the way as she entered the room. She flipped the light switch and headed straight for the desk, not even remotely concerned about the silent alarm or anyone who might notice her presence.

The inbox that sat atop the heavily polished workspace was neat and orderly: only one file sat askew, like it had been tossed there at the end of the day, when it's owner had decided enough was enough and a glass of wine at home sounded better than pigeonholing this last tedious bit business.

Cassidy figured that was the sort of thing that happened when your carefully laid plans suddenly went awry. She grinned a little, taking full credit for the upheaval her presence had caused.

The filing cabinets were not locked. Cassidy browsed leisurely through the files in each drawer; they were conveniently alphabetized so It did not take long before she had found what she was looking for. There it was, filed under *R* for his adoptive parent's surname.

She stared at the tan coloured folder in her hands for a moment before she took a deep breath and, nodding her head, for she know in her heart what she was doing was right, she opened it. Pinned to the inside flap with a bright blue paperclip was exactly what she had been looking for. *Those impossible lashes.* She slipped it out from beneath its confines and replaced the folder back into its slot. She flopped into the ergonomic office chair and began to methodically search through the desk drawers until she found the item she sought. A simple envelope, a simple inclusion; it felt heavy in her hands. Sealing the picture inside, she grabbed a sharpie and scrawled *Ella – He IS Loved* across the front in her bold cursive script.

This one last time she would go through the portal. One last time would she set foot on Lotus Lorea; a brief excursion to repay a kindness, to try and somehow right a wrong when her options were limited. It was the only way she knew how.

Errand completed, Cassidy stood in front of the portal entrance, wracked with indecision. The fine hairs at the back of her neck and on her arms were raised in response to the thrum of the portal. Even now, she could feel it, the inexplicable pull of its siren song.

It would not take much to put an end to it all. There weren't any people in the building right now. If she took it down, the destruction could easily be linked to the earlier explosion on Fraser Place. Random acts of violence that were becoming more and more common these days. Some minor faction who was angry about something. There was *always* someone angry about something these days.

She could think of no other way to break the link, to cut the cord. Could she really go through with it though?

The ways of old.

The words echoed around the empty room, as though someone had spoken them out loud. Perhaps she had.

No, she would not be able to bear that burden, knowing that she would leave them with virtually no other choice. Cassidy backed out into the corridor and closed the door behind her with an air of finality. She nodded once, her decision made. And then she walked away.

There was a lightness in her step as the weight was lifted off of her shoulders. She had done what she thought was best. And there was no burden left for her to carry.

She glanced ruefully at the office door she had obliterated a short while ago. She shrugged. Collateral damage. Sorry not sorry.

As she pivoted to exit the building, a sense of whimsy overcame her. She thought, why not? If for nothing other than coming full circle, putting an end to her adventure. She stepped back in through what was left of the office door, chuckling to herself as she kicked her way through the debris. She slid open the office window and hoisted herself up to the ledge. She swung her legs around and, without so much as a backward glance, she dropped to the ground outside, landing lithely on her feet. Still in a crouch, she paused. And in a moment of uncharacteristic charity, Cassidy turned back around and shut the window behind her before she ran off in a crouch, heading towards the gap in the fence.

Taking a deep lungful of the cool evening air, Cassidy shivered as her body struggled to adjust to the change in core temperature between here and Lotus Lorea. Cassidy picked her way through the maze of fences and trees, stumbling through the darkness, tripping over rocks and exposed tree roots. She thought longingly of a hot shower and a generous pour of red; the peace and quiet of her own home.

One foot in front of the other. It kept her going.

Finally, she emerged from within the woods. She was back to where she had started; before she knew what she would come up against. She peered suspicious from behind the Carina Heights welcome sign, always on alert and—

Darn it.

Her car had been towed.

And it was a long walk home.

CHAPTER TWELVE

Back in her old bed at last, sleep had found her quickly, and so had the dream. The dream unfolded rather pleasantly at first, Cassidy was playing fetch with a Labrador Retriever, the golden dog bounding joyfully though a sweet-smelling meadow in agile pursuit of a bright yellow tennis ball. The grass was tall, fragrant and a beautiful emerald green, still damp with morning dew. The sun was shining brightly and Cassidy had to use a hand to shield her eyes. In the distance, a red and white checkered picnic blanket had been spread out on the ground and Cassidy could see sandwiches, salads, fried chicken, chips and cookies laid out, waiting to be eaten. The dog returned to her feet, dropped the ball and demanded her attention. He barked happily and waited, tail wagging, panting in anticipation.

Somehow Cassidy knew that his name was Fred.

Cassidy picked up the ball and launched it in the direction of an old oak tree; it disappeared amongst the grass, and Fred zoomed after it. His pure joy at such a simple game made Cassidy laugh, a carefree sound that echoed in the stillness of the field.

She'd definitely had worse dreams.

A low rumble of thunder drew her gaze skyward: deeply bruised Cumulonimbus clouds steamrolled towards her, bringing with them a cool, charged breeze and a whiff of rain and ozone. A thunderstorm was brewing. She looked around for an umbrella. She did not have one.

As dreams are often wont to do, time shifted swiftly and Cassidy soon found herself sitting Criss-Cross Applesauce on the picnic blanket. Fred had not returned with the ball and she whipped her head around frantically, searching for the errant pup. She couldn't lose him. Thunder rumbled overhead; the storm had moved in quickly. Cassidy looked down to find herself holding a triangle sandwich. It was ham and cheese. There was a plate on her lap filled with lush raspberries. The juice from the berries had seeped through the flimsy paper of the plate. Red stains had spread across the white linen pants she was wearing. She swiped at it ineffectively with a paper napkin.

"Would you like some lemonade, Miss Cane?"

She startled at the sound of the voice, having assumed she was alone in the dream now that Fred had gone missing. She turned towards the sound.

"Dr. Gamgee!"

"Would you like some lemonade, Miss Cane?"

For a second time he offered her an empty pitcher, his voice low and devoid of intonation or emotion; his gaze was fixed on a point somewhere above her head.

"Dr. G, are you feeling okay? There's nothing in your jug."

"Lemonade. We need to make the lemonade."

"Sure. Let me help you with that!" She tried to get up but found that her movements were sluggish, as though she were walking through a pool of thick syrup.

"We need water to make the lemonade. You have the water."

"What… I don't…"

"THE WATER!" he shouted. An intense flash of lighting ignited the sky and suddenly Gamgee was right next to her, his eyes frantic and boring straight into hers. He thrust the jug insistently into her hands.

"THE WATER MAKES THE LEMONADE AND THE LEMONADE QUENCHES OUR THIRST!"

Cassidy tried to back away from the onslaught, shaking her head in confusion and fear. *Wake up! Wake up!*

"SAVE US ALL, CASSIDY! GIVE US THE WATER! WE WILL DIE OF THIRST!"

The voices multiplied, rising in volume and ferocity, as behind Gamgee there winked into existence every single person Cassidy had ever known and loved in her life. Before her very eyes, one by one, they began to shrivel, dry up, turn to dust.

The air heavy with the ashes of her friends and family, Cassidy coughed and blinked rapidly to clear her vision. Gamgee shuffled closer towards her, his voice rasping, "Water, water!" His lower jaw slackened, widened and his eyes sunk back into his head; Gamgee reached for Cassidy imploringly, holding out the jug. Cassidy tried to back away, she closed her eyes, willing herself to just wake the hell up. She heard a dog yelp in the distance, a cry of fear and pain. Her eyes popped open and suddenly she was face to face with the nightmare Gamgee. As his fetid breath washed over her, an overwhelming odour of sickness and decomposition, a deafening explosion of thunder rocked the meadow and Cassidy exploded from her bed, breathing heavily and covered in sweat. She threw back the blankets and jumped to her feet. Stumbling to the ensuite, she accidentally knocked over the toothbrush holder and soap dispenser in her haste to grab the tumbler next to the bathroom sink. She ran the tap until cool clear water overflowed the cup and then she drank it down.

It wasn't difficult to interpret *that* dream.

Cassidy refilled the glass and, leaning against the vanity, gulped it greedily. She splashed water on her face and stood there, dripping, staring at herself in the mirror.

There was no amount of water that would be able to slake her thirst tonight.

And she was never eating pizza before bed again.

CHAPTER THIRTEEN

Cassidy marched into the office, takeout coffee cup grasped firmly in hand, the highly recognizable mermaid logo of the coffee shop emblazoned across the front. She took a nourishing slurp of the hot frothy concoction and smacked her lips in satisfaction. It was no *jaroot*, that was true, but the latte was fantastic enough in its own right. And she definitely needed all the caffeine she could get. She dropped her messenger bag on the floor of the office, next to her desk, and placed her laptop case carefully next to it. She slipped her new jacket off her shoulders and slung it on the back of her chair. She cleared a small space for the coffee cup amongst the wild disarray of her desk and sat down to mournfully regard the mess in front of her.

Where did she even start.

She dragged her dishevelled hair into a low ponytail, swiped a hand across her face, and began to rummage through the pile of paperwork and mail that had accumulated in the inbox on her desk. Though most of it would end up in the recycling bin, there was an invitation to speak at the International Conference on Archaeological

Anthropology and Human Cultural Experience in Kuala Lumpur, Malaysia that Cassidy filed away for later consideration; there was a thank you card from Annie and Ximena for the baby shower gift, and also several memos from the department head asking if she had picked a research assistant for the summer based on the student resumes he had forwarded to her. Resumes? Cassidy made a face at the stacks of files and paperwork and uncorrected term papers on her desk.

Probably under there… somewhere.

Restlessness overcame her. She pulled the elastic out of her hair and swept the locks to one side. She leaned back in her chair, clasping her coffee cup in hand as though it were a life preserver; she sipped and speculated.

Maybe it was time for her to get away for a little bit; a getaway that was a *vacation*, one she planned on her own terms where there were no tasks to complete, no ulterior motives. When was the last time she'd gone on a holiday?

Cassidy needed this destination to be a faraway place where she could get out and explore; she wanted to try new things and meet new people. Rest and relaxation was not the most important factor, so beaches were not up for consideration. Cassidy popped up from the swivel chair and grabbed a well worn map of the world from the box that sat beside her bookshelf. She smoothed it out and tacked it quickly to the wall, visualizing all the places she had travelled around the world... and around other worlds as well. There were still so many endless possibilities.

From atop a filing cabinet, Cassidy picked up a single,

brass tipped dart from amongst the trinkets and artifacts she kept there, those she had collected on her travels, things that were dear to her, that brought back fond memories of her many exploits. A cheeky grin played across her lips. She crossed the room and turned to face the map. Closing her eyes, she took a deep breath and threw the dart, aiming nowhere in particular, dreaming solely of escape. She heard a satisfying *thunk* as the sharp point buried itself deep in the dense wood of the wall. She drew closer to the map and squinted at the tiny Canadian island her dart had landed on. She sounded it out, the name rolling off her tongue: Newfoundland. The shape of its rugged coastline appealed to her. She slipped her laptop out of its case.

A quick internet search showed bright, jelly bean coloured row houses; there were zip lines excursions, world class restaurants, and incredible hiking trails. She'd already heard talk of the Viking settlements in L'Anse aux Meadows from her peers and grinned in anticipation of what she might discover there. There were breathtaking ocean views and a wild, untouched beauty. She quickly booked a flight, more excited than she had been about anything in quite some time.

A brisk knock at the door was an unwelcome intrusion as she daydreamed about her upcoming jaunt, but was not entirely unexpected at a busy university. Cassidy closed the lid of her laptop, sliding it back into its satchel. A second knock sounded before she had a chance to respond. She sighed.

"Come in."

Doctor Gamgee poked his head around the door, a

broad grin on his face. Cassidy was impressed that he had paused long enough to knock and wait this time, rather than just barge in as was his normal entrance style. It was some progress at least.

"Miss Cane. So glad to have you back with us! May I come in for a moment?" he said, already making his way through the door and into the room.

"Of course," Cassidy replied dryly.

"I trust you have, err, recuperated from your little… experience the other night?"

Cassidy had had to fabricate a story to explain, well, everything that had happened to her. There were lots of questions. Her car had still not been recovered. She'd called numerous towing companies but none had a record of her vehicle in their lots. Her missing phone, which had now been replaced, had required the distribution of a new phone number to her colleagues and friends. And then there were the injuries she'd sustained. No amount of makeup or long sleeves could hide the still healing scrapes and bruises that peppered her face and hands.

She tried to keep her story simple, Occam's razor and all that jazz. She stuck with the story she'd already set up in her text messages to Gamgee, when she had found herself searching through Carina Heights for Ella and Everlee. Wracked with insomnia and feeling a little out of sorts, she had gone for a drive. Finding herself in a part of town that was new to her, she'd made a stupid split second decision and had left her car to walk around and explore. Silly her, she had become hopelessly lost in an unfamiliar area. A stumble in the darkness explained away her injuries. She had dropped her phone and keys, had not been able to find them. People had no reason to question it, no reason to not believe her. She was, after all, stalwart and trustworthy to a fault.

Cassidy was fully aware that Gamgee knew that there was more to her story. She could tell by the way he looked at her that he was confused as to why she had not gone to him straight away to tell the whole sordid tale. But he did not press for details. For that she was grateful. Perhaps she would share it with him eventually. She just wasn't ready yet. How could she even explain all that had come to pass while she was away? There were still some things she could not even explain to herself.

She did not have a sample of the water from The Lotus Fountain to turn over to him. Cassidy suspected that, in Gamgee's mind, her mission would ultimately have to be declared a failure. How could she explain her reasoning to Doctor Gamgee? He was a man who dealt with data and cold hard facts; emotion was something that was very rarely a factor used in his rationale. Cassidy hated to disappoint people and she vowed to make it up to him if given the chance. She hoped to have the opportunity again, despite the still underlying anger over the fact that he had not been open and forthright with her about the portal at the agency to begin with.

CHAPTER FOURTEEN

She'd never actually had a need for one before but there was always a first time for everything, especially when you were Cassidy Cane.

As the bank manager left the room to allow her a modicum of privacy, as the door closed softly behind him, Cassidy eyed the safety deposit box on the table in front of her with a mixture of relief and dread. It was an entirely last resort option, but it was the best solution she could come up with in the final moments before she left Plainsfield again. Who knew when she'd be back again this time around.

She gingerly placed her messenger bag on the table next to the box, flipped it open and paused, her fingers tapping against the canvas flap. Well, there *was* one other option. She bit her lip, torn; her thoughts a jumbled jigsaw of pieces she wasn't sure she could ever put back together again. No, it had to be this way. Final decision. She simply could not bring herself to destroy something of such utter significance but she *was* determined to keep it out of the wrong hands.

The book went in first, gently. It's faded viridian cover

nearly blending in with the slate grey of the box. Next she took a small package from the depths of her bag and held it aloft with both hands so that it caught the light. She observed closely as the fluid inside the small, airtight capsule, enclosed inside a vacuum sealed bag, reflected the glare of the overhead florescent bulbs. It sure appeared innocuous enough. Cassidy smirked. She knew the difference though. Oh boy, did she ever.

It was her sample of the Lotus potion.

She placed the parcel inside the box, right next to the book, and locked it up with a decisive turn of the wrist. She slid the coffer back inside its compartment and pocketed the key. Done.

She picked up her bag, turned around and walked out the door.

She did not look back.

EPILOGUE

"Come quick!" Zikix yelled, his cries echoing through the hall of the solitary confinement wing of the Xik'en world penitentiary. He bellowed with such force that it seemed to kick the sawdust up from the floor. His voice was panicked but forceful -- the voice of someone in charge but faced with a new, surprising situation.

His tail flicked with agitation, twitching this way and that as he paced.

Kizix stepped into the shadowed dark of the hall, holding the low ceiling with one hand as he bent and peered in. Kizix was taller than most Xik'en by a foot and a half, and often had to watch his head in this way. He waited for his serpentine eyes to adjust to the light, his scaled skin twitching.

The hallway before Kizix was narrow, with cells on either side. There was a single light hanging from overhead casting strange, oblong shadows on the walls all around.

"What is it?" Kizix called, straightening the collar of his guard uniform. It wasn't made for a Xik'en of his size and was always too tight.

"It's the warm-blood!" Zikix yelled in return. "It's not

breathing!" Before Kizix even had a chance to respond again, Zikix took out his emergency key card and pushed it against the reader of the warm-blood prisoner -- named Tallis' -- cell. A red light turned on in the hall behind Kizix.

Tallis was passed out, face down in the sawdust, which was stuck in his black, shoulder-length hair, and sprawled out, his limbs looking like spider-legs. He was dressed in the same black shirt and jeans he'd worn the day he was brought in, now soiled with mammal stench. The sawdust was everywhere, and Zikix was instantly worried that he'd had a seizure. He grabbed Tallis by the shoulders and pulled him over onto his back. His lips had begun to turn blue.

Kizix ran down the hall, stopping briefly at a hand washing station in the center of the hall and scrubbing. He picked up a portable light from a dispensary beneath and flicked it on, its bright rectangle shimmering out as he made his way towards the action. He lowered it when Zikix held up his hand to block his eyes.

Zikix motioned Kizix to look at the lips. "They're not supposed to do that, are they?"

Kizix shook his head. "No, they aren't." He paused. "Do you know warm-blood CPR?" He got down next to Tallis and placed his head on his chest.

"No I don't know warm-blood CPR! Why would I know that?"

"There's supposed to be someone on every shift that knows it!"

"Take it up with scheduling!" Zikix snapped. "What are you doing?"

"The heartbeat is strong." He placed two hands over Tallis' solar plexus. "I'll push. I think this is where its lungs are. You breathe into it?"

"You expect me to touch its mouth?"

"Just do it!"

Zikix sighed and bent down, hovering over the strange shape that was the mammal's breathing orifice, and mentally prepared himself to place his own over it.

Kizix pushed down on Tallis' chest.

At once, a small, thin stress ball flew up from his mouth and struck Zikix in the eye!

"Aah!" Zikix screamed, the shock affecting him more than the impact. He splayed back from it, wiping the saliva from his eye.

Kizix's head snapped around to Tallis, just in time for Tallis to bring up his fist and knock him to the ground.

Tallis coughed, struggling to his feet. He found his stress ball in the hay, picked it up, then took the keycard from Kizix. He then turned to Zikix and held out his hand. "I'll take your Branch."

Zikix stared at Tallis for a long moment, his mouth twisted in a sneer. Reluctantly, he reached up and removed the Branch of Languages from the side of his face and held it out to Tallis.

The golden nanotech wires cradling slivers of green Vao stones shimmered, reflecting in Tallis' hungry eyes. He took it and placed it along the left side of his face, whereas Zikix had worn it on the right. He felt it become alive. Moving like a snake, it slipped along Tallis' jawline, its peak disappearing into the hair above his left ear. A comfortable warmth replaced the tingle it had started with.

"Thank you," Tallis said with an all-too-polite tone, turning and leaving his cell and shutting the door behind him.

Zikix could only watch as he went, up the stairs and into the main area of the prison. Soon after, alarms sounded.

ACKNOWLEDGEMENTS

The authors would like to pay special thanks to the *Slipstreamers* committee at Engen Books, including Amanda Labonté, Matthew LeDrew, AJ Ryan, Ellen Curtis, Erin Vance, and, Lauralana Dunne.

Without their tireless efforts, none of this would have been possible.

Special thanks to this episode's editor, Ali House.

Nicole Little would also like to thank her husband Sébastien and daughters Bridget and Suzie who have shown her that needing peace and quiet to write is clearly a myth. Their continued support and encouragement have made all the difference.

COMING SOON!
PLAGUE OF THE DREAMLESS
BY JD RYOT & JENNIFER SHELBY!

The next incredible episode of Slipstreamers, Plague of the Dreamless, will be available soon, written with Jennifer Shelby!

When Cassidy ignores a common cold while venturing to a new world, the accidentally sets off a chain reaction that threatens all life on it! Can she set things right before it's too late?

SPECIAL BONUS STORIES!

We're pleased to present nine additional stories from this episode's incredible award-winning co-author, Nicole Little.

Nicole Little is one of only a handful of authors to be included in three or more *From the Rock* collections, earning her the title of Rocker, and is recognized as a gifted crafter of short fiction.

From the Rock is a series of anthologies from Engen Books exploring young adult takes on a variety of genres from authors around Atlantic Canada.

In addition to reprinting many of her From the Rock entries, this collection also includes her award-winning story *Sweet Sixteen* and several other pieces of flash fiction submitted for consideration in the Kit Sora Flash Fiction contest.

SWEET SIXTEEN

Bridget always felt a connection to her mother at the beach. Perhaps the rhythm of the waves caressing the shore reminded her of the rhythm of the womb; it was, after all, the only memory she had of her.

Abandoned at the water's edge, no more than a few hours old, her frantic newborn cries had attracted the attention of a pod of mermaids swimming nearby. She'd heard the story a million times: how their songs had soothed her and how, wrapped in their gossamer tresses and lulled by the lap of the water, she'd fallen asleep in their arms. Enraptured with this tiny human, they'd persuaded Neptune to grant just one request. He had cupped the baby's tiny feet and bestowed upon her a most precious gift.

And now she has returned to the threshold of the ocean that had nearly been her end but, in a peculiar twist of fate, turned out to be her beginning. On the cusp of her sixteenth birthday, she must choose, as so many have done before her, to walk upon the land or remain in the sea.

At midnight, breaking the surface softly, she's surprised to see a solitary woman walking along the beach. She watches as the woman stops, places a single flower on the sand, and walks away. Bridget's breath catches, but she knows now what she must do. Casting one last glance back at what might have been, she dives beneath the waves and returns to what has always been.

SQUID WARS

"Delivery for Edward Allen Farris." The message flashed in bright red letters.

"That's me!"

Ed placed his palm on the scanner where the delivery-bot indicated and grabbed the small cardboard box when it dropped from the slot. He hadn't ordered anything, and he didn't often receive unsolicited mail, but he did like surprises! He turned it over and over in his hands and gave it a light shake. A muffled rattle from within piqued his curiosity.

There was no return address.

He closed the door, grabbed scissors from the junk drawer in the kitchen, and deftly sliced through the tape. He pawed through the sea of trappings in search of buried treasure.

"What the flip?" he muttered under his breath. *GROW A FRIEND!* declared the retro, overly bright, child-centric packaging. Mystified, he read aloud from the instructions on the back: *"Place your egg in water and watch it hatch! Within 24 hours, you will have a new best friend! Add more water as necessary."*

Ed laughed mirthlessly. This was a joke right? Who in the world would send such a thing to a forty-year-old man? He tossed the toy on the counter and stalked out of the room, disappointed and oddly irritated. He sat at his desk and tried to concentrate.

But his attention waned.

It was 11PM; Ed stood at the kitchen sink, rinsing an empty wine glass. Finally, admitting defeat, he got down on his knees to rummage through the cupboards. He emerged, triumphant, with a large bowl in hand. Seconds later he was standing at the counter observing the opalescent-toned egg as it wobbled and bobbed in its incubator of tepid tap water. He was embarrassed to admit it, even to himself, but he was intrigued; a certain childish curiosity had overtaken him. He sighed in resignation and went to bed.

***

Ed sat straight up in bed, his heart beating a wild tattoo beneath his chest; his legs tangled tightly in a twisted sheet. Flipping on the lamp next to his bed, he strained to hear what had woken him. It had not been a dream. It had been much too loud, echoing even now above the rush of blood in his ears. As the minutes languidly ticked past, Ed, mustering courage, crept from the bed to the doorway. Met with silence there, he tiptoed stealthily down the hall. No burglars or boogiemen greeted him in the small lounge, so he continued into the kitchen.

Dappled in moonlight, the alabaster bowl upon the counter immediately drew Ed's attention. *Needs more water*, he thought. Mechanically he filled a measuring cup with liquid from the tap, poured it carefully into the bowl and watched the egg weave, dip, and dive in its replenished fluids. Within minutes, he was back in bed, his breathing slow and deep. Asleep.

Whether or not he noticed the long crack running the length of the shell is anyone's guess.

***

Bleary eyes blinked tiredly over the rim of a chipped blue coffee mug emblazoned with the proverb *Edit or Regret It*. Ed's internal clock would not allow him to sleep past 615am even though it was a Saturday; even though he felt strangely exhausted. It was as though he hadn't slept well at all. He yawned widely, ran a hand over his chin stubble; the entire day stretched out ahead of him and he wondered, idly, if it was worth shaving for. He tossed the dregs of his coffee into a potted plant beside him (a plant that somehow seemed to thrive despite his indifference) and, leaving the mug on a side table, he meandered upstairs to get dressed. He was spitting toothpaste into the sink when he heard the muffled sound of glass breaking. He wiped his chin hurriedly and fled the bathroom.

The mug, his favorite, lay in jagged shards on the floor.

"What in the world?" he sputtered.

There was no draft of wind, no mischievous pet to knock it over; he was sure he hadn't left the mug near the edge. He sighed, took a knee, and began to pick up the broken pieces, cursing elaborately under his breath. He wasn't paying much mind to anything other than the task at hand. So when the oily black tentacle whipped out from beneath the recliner and wrapped itself around Ed's wrist, well, let's just say, it definitely got his attention.

Ed had finally met his new best friend.

***

"What's the word, Sook?"

Roxy Buckles sashayed her way into the office. It was 10am and she reeked of scotch and late-night shenanigans.

Suki Kwan, who'd been fielding irate calls all morning, wrinkled her nose in distaste. "You need a shower, Roxy."

Roxy sniffed an armpit. "I didn't have time to go home last night... or this morning. Either way, I'll freshen up before my first meeting." She stopped mid stride. "When is my first meeting again?"

"Two hours ago," Suki responded with wide eyed innocence.

Roxy cringed.

Suki grinned. "You can relax. I moved all your appointments. Ethel-Beth Lester will be here in ..." she glanced at the time, "... twenty minutes. Her husband ran off a Witchlet again. She's afraid they'll eat him this time. Go spray yourself with something. There's a coffee on your desk."

Roxy ran a hand through her golden halo of curls and flashed Suki a grateful grin. "Thanks, Sook. What would I do without you?"

"Die probably," Suki muttered as Roxy slammed the door of the inner office.

Suki was feeding handwritten notes into the Transcripto Scanner when she heard an alarm reverberate throughout the room. She froze for a few seconds before glancing around to make sure she wasn't imagining things. It wasn't a sound she heard often in the office. Oh, yes they received thousands of alerts a year but *never* on *that* line.

Suki smashed the acknowledge button, printed the specs, then wheeled frantically to the inner office door. Bursting in, Suki caught Roxy as she was just about to spritz herself with a can of Shower-On-The-Go. The can hit the floor and rolled beneath the desk.

"Jeepers, Suki! You scared the life out of me!"

"Rox. There's a problem ... um ... *over there*." She widened her eyes dramatically. There was only one *over there*.

"Earth?! Really? Shoot. What is it?"

"Here." Suki handed Roxy the small paper printout.

"Flunk me dead! It's a LanQuid! This is ... this is extinction level!" Roxy bent to grab the can of Shower-On-The-Go and called over her shoulder to Suki, her voice hard and resolute: "Cancel my appointments, Sook, and fire up the Zip Ship. "

Suki sighed in resignation, thinking mournfully of the calendar she'd only just rearranged. She began transmitting instructions to the Bots down in transport. The Zip Ship, used for short interstellar jaunts, would be prepped and ready to go whenever Roxy was.

Within minutes, Roxy was on the tarmac. She climbed up and settled herself into the pilot seat of the Zip Ship, pleased but not surprised, to see that Suki had already programmed the coordinates into the navigation system. She quickly did her pre-flight checks and secured her safety harness. Satisfied that everything was as it should be, she took a deep breath: it was go time.

Urging the Zip Ship onward at top speed, Roxy mentally reviewed everything she knew about LanQuids. Greedy as they were for anything liquid, they'd driven their home planet into an irreversible drought. Intercepted before they could travel to other solar systems, they'd been ordered to remain in situ by the Planetary Regulation Committee. They'd eventually died off.

Or so everyone thought.

A LanQuid on Earth would be utterly disastrous.

***

Eventually Ed stopped screaming.

The tentacle had retreated back beneath the chair. Ed wondered – hoped that maybe he'd imagined the whole thing?

He took a deep breath. Then: "Hello?"

A small squeak in reply.

"Can… can you come out where I can see you? What *are* you?"

Silence. No movement. But then, slowly, something that Ed could never have imagined in his wildest dreams scuttled out from beneath his favorite recliner. It resembled a small squid; if that squid had been drenched in motor oil. It was obsidian-black, aqueous in appearance and many-tentacled. It twitched and writhed in constant movement, as though furiously seeking… something. Two large moist eyes, centered perfectly upon its countenance, peered curiously out at Ed from above a small, sharp beak-like protuberance. It squawked and Ed felt his bladder tremble.

"What do you want?!" Ed finally croaked.

A sound which might have been a cough emanated from behind the beak and suddenly Ed knew. "Water?"

The gleeful noise that followed was all the answer he needed.

Ed's new friend was splashing ecstatically around the bathtub; the bathroom floor was splattered. As was Ed for that matter. And if Ed's eyes didn't deceive him, it had grown at least a few inches. It *had* consumed a considerable amount of bath water though.

Ed hated calling it *It*.

"We need a name for you, little buddy." Two large liquid eyes blinked at him quizzically. Ed thought for a minute. "What about Inky? Wait... Cal! That one's short for Calamari!" Ed chuckled to himself. The creature didn't seem to find it very funny. "Okay, Cal it is!"

Ed turned on the tap, adjusted the temperature. Cal squealed loudly in delight. "Wow. You sure do like water, hey?! I'll fill it back up for you then!"

***

It had been a very long time since Roxy had navigated through Earth's atmosphere. Sweat ran down the sides of her face as she felt the craft vibrate and shudder beneath her hands; she breathed an audible sigh of relief when the Zip Ship finally touched down on terra firma. Night had fallen over the small town of Port Sebastian. There was little chance of getting lost but Roxy grabbed her map-nav anyways before exiting the craft. Leaning against the Zip, her breath forming a mist in front of her lips, she studied it closely, using her intuition to narrow down the areas she suspected that the LanQuid might target. She memorized the street names and jammed the device into her pocket. She set off at a steady pace.

The sound of Roxy's combat boots scuffing against the

asphalt echoed loudly on the otherwise silent thoroughfare of Ripley Avenue. She ambled down Ripley, then
left onto Connor; eyes constantly scanning the houses,
cloaked though they were in darkness; sleepy and still
at this time of night – not even a curtain twitched. Roxy
stuffed her hands in her pockets, her fingers brushing the
map-nav; she suppressed a small shiver. The jacket she
was wearing, though perfect for the year-round balmy
weather on Aurora, was wildly inadequate in this chilly
autumn breeze.

Thus far, Earth wasn't living up to the hype.

Rounding the corner onto Leonard, Roxy was beginning to doubt her instincts. There should have been some
sign by now surely… unless she was wrong. It didn't happen often but, though she was loathed to admit it, it wasn't
entirely outside the realm of possibility.

The screech that split the night air had Roxy reaching
for her weapon – a multifunctional tool that, with a simple
spin of a dial, could adapt and challenge any hostile being large or small. Roxy fell into a crouch, her senses on
alert. Another scream pierced the silence. Loud enough
that Roxy could pinpoint its location: 14 Leonard Way. A
blue, nondescript house with a tidy front yard complete
with white picket fence. Roxy crept closer, read the name
printed on the mailbox: *Farris*.

A thunderous crash. The upstairs light went out.

Bingo.

***

Ed returned from a day out running errands. Night
came early this time of year; he flicked the lights on as
he walked through the house, not particularly concerned

with his carbon footprint. He was tired and hungry. He wanted a sandwich and a beer in front of the TV followed by an early night.

You know what they say about best laid plans.

Yawning enormously, Ed plodded up the stairs, a small bag of shrimp in hand. He'd grabbed some earlier at the supermarket, thinking it might be a nice treat for his new mate Cal. He strolled distractedly into the guest bathroom and stopped short. The bathtub was empty. And completely dry. A few hours beforehand it had been filled nearly to the brim and had contained one tiny squid-like creature. Absurdly, the toilet bowl was also empty. Ed stood there for a few moments, blinking stupidly, his mind processing the scene; the forgotten bag drooped limply by his side.

A deafening shriek made the floor beneath his feet tremble. The bag of seafood tumbled onto the bathroom rug as Ed flinched and covered his ears. Sprinting from the bathroom, Ed soon found himself face to face with Cal. A grown up Cal. A rather large, rather menacing Cal.

It towered over Ed by at least two feet and was nearly four times as wide. Spittle dripped from its beak as it squawked and sputtered, slithering slowly down the hall toward Ed, its girth brushing against the framed photos on the walls. A picture of an elder Farris hit the floor and smashed. An antique side table had much the same fate. But Cal did not slow. The beast's bulbous ebony head swayed gelatinously as it moved, its red-tinged eyes squinted but remained focused in the bright of the light spilling out of the bathroom.

It charged.

Ed screamed.

And that's when all hell broke loose.

***

"Who the hell are you?" Ed screamed.

"Roxy Buckles: Intergalactic Exterminator. And I'm here to save your ass!"

The woman, who had seemed to appear out of nowhere in Ed's upstairs hallway, was holding a weapon that his brain just could not comprehend. She moved with a fluidity he associated with dancers or perhaps swimmers, dodging wild swiping tentacles without blinking an eye. She fell to one knee and took aim at the creature formerly known as Cal.

"Get down!!" she ordered. Ed hit the ground and rolled through the still open doorway of the bathroom.

From the hallway came the classic sounds of a tussle: grunting, and flesh pounding flesh. Ed cringed as the din reached a crescendo: glass shattered and a torrent of curses reached his ears. Under different circumstances, Ed might have blushed over such colorful language. Then, a peculiar whirring noise erupted, like thousands of bees had descended on Leonard Way.

"Cover your eyes!"

Ed barely heard the warning over the cacophony of noise but did not hesitate to do as he was told. A superhuman wail filled the house and the hair on the back of Ed's neck stood on end. A violent shudder and he felt the floor ripple beneath his trembling body... and everything went black.

"Hey! Can you hear me?"

The softly spoken words penetrated his subconscious and Ed's eyes blinked open. "Am I dead?"

She chuckled softly. "No, Mr. Farris, I think you'll be okay. You're safe now. Though you'll need to do some renovations. And also probably take a shower."

Ed raised a hand in front of his face. It was covered in a thick black gore. Raising himself slightly on his elbows, wincing as his lower back protested, he saw that his entire self was covered in the sludge. And the walls. And the floor.

And also the woman crouched next to him. She looked like *Carrie* at the prom… if they'd dumped motor oil on her instead of blood. She ran a hand across her mouth, turned her head to the side and spat.

"Gosh, this stuff gets everywhere."

"Um. What exactly is this *stuff*? Is this … is this *Cal*?"

"Cal?" she questioned. "This is the ichor from the Lan-Quid I just blasted to smithereens out there in your hallway."

"Lan… Quid?"

"Yes. That's what I said. An invasive species. We thought they were extinct!" She seemed delighted, given the circumstances.

"But he was so tiny this morning."

"Let me guess, you gave it water?"

"Of course. He seemed to really love it!"

"They sure do, Mr. Farris, sure do. It's absolutely gluttonous when it comes to liquid. The more it drinks, the bigger it gets. It can decimate an entire planet in *days*. Especially a planet like this one."

Ed felt a little twinge of sadness. So much for a new best friend.

"Sorry, in all the chaos I missed it. What did you say your name was?"

"Roxy Buckles." She extended a hand and pulled Ed to his feet.

"And you, hunt things, kill them? Things like Cal? I mean, the LanQuid?"

"That's my job!"

"I can't thank you enough! You saved my life!"

"All in a day's work, Mr. Farris." She smiled and glanced down at a small device on her left wrist that was emitting an insistent beep. She grabbed a towel off the rack – it seemed to have escaped the worst of the slaughter -- and swiped at the face of the electronic. "Sorry to cut this short, but I have a meeting about a Witchlet that I cannot miss."

Before Ed could react, she was gone out the door.

It had been the wildest day of Ed's entire life.

***

He'd stayed at a hotel for a few days while the cleaners came in. Thankfully they didn't ask a lot of questions. Ed didn't have a lot of answers anyways. It would take a while longer to repair the walls and floor upstairs, but the house was habitable enough.

He was sitting at the kitchen table, drinking a cup of coffee when the doorbell rang.

"Delivery for Edward Allen Farris."

"That's me!"

Ed placed his palm on the scanner where the deliverybot indicated and grabbed the small cardboard box when it dropped from the slot.

He already had the bowl ready on the kitchen counter.

But maybe not so much water this time.

A SIGN OF SPRING

"A cup of tea for your kindness?" asked the old lady.

"Thank you." Lisette gladly accepted the steaming beverage into her freezing hands. An involuntary shiver ran through her.

"It's the least I can do my child. To repay you for coming to my rescue."

Lisette sat at the old fashion Formica table, enveloped in the scent of cinnamon and cloves. She'd been shovelling snow for the elderly in her neighborhood ever since the record breaking snowfall two days before. It was, however, the first time she'd been invited inside anyone's home.

"This tea is very tasty!" Lisette offered. A bold-faced lie, as she struggled to fill the awkward silence.

The woman beamed: "My own special blend!" She turned then and gazed outside with longing, "It's very difficult to get around in the snow at my age. I long for a sign of Spring."

Lisette nodded sympathetically.

Having now consumed what she thought was an acceptable amount of tea, she murmured: "I should go. There's a few more driveways."

"Of course! Thank you again for your help."

Lisette retrieved her shovel and headed down the driveway. An uneasy rumble in her stomach stopped her in her tracks.

She saw the woman watching her intently through the window.

She waved.

Lisette hiccupped, her eyes going wide; she bent at the waist as an intense fluttering sensation swamped her insides. She coughed and retched and suddenly, from her mouth, erupted a stream of multicolored butterflies.

Inside the house, the old woman smiled.

THE BARREL OF THE FABRISHEMSHIRE

The large oval-shaped metallic object that stood, half buried in the ground, in the middle of the town square had been there for as long as anyone in Fabrishemshire could remember. In fact, the square had actually been built *around* the object.

The townsfolk held a certain begrudging respect for it.

Most of them were afraid not to.

Lysander Drake, aged 8 and a half, was a precocious child. On days when her mother went to the farmer's market Lysander requested she'd be left in the gardens of the square. She liked to observe the bumble bees as they buzzed amongst the flowers and all the busy people who walked past. Or so she insisted.

In reality she wanted to watch The Barrel.

It had *always* been called The Barrel but not officially so until 1961 when Walter Peabody, having tended the gardens all through his teens, placed a hand painted sign at the foot of the object:

`The Barrel of Fabrishemshire. DO NOT TOUCH.`

And there it still remained, faded but readable. Walter was now just a few short months' shy of retirement.

On this particular day, the 18th of July, the sun was high and bright in the sky. Amelia Drake wheeled her young daughter along the cobbled path, placed a kiss upon her flaxen head and locked the wheels of her chair next to a Bougainvillea. She paused for a moment. She was hesitant to leave the girl alone here but Lys would hear tell of nothing else.

"I'll be back soon my dear."

"Ok Mummy! Goodbye!"

With a slight, bemused shake of her head, Amelia set off at a steady pace for Athlone Place where the market was held each weekend.

Lysander listened to the receding footsteps of her mother. When the sound had faded, she glanced over her shoulder to be sure, and then unlocked the brakes on her wheelchair, pushing herself closer to The Barrel.

It towered over young Lysander. With a curious eye she took in its smooth polished surface, how it somehow absorbed rather than reflected the midday sun. It emitted a mild low-frequency hum that everyone else seemed unaffected by. Lysander felt it though. It thrummed along her veins. And the closer she was to it, the stronger the drone became.

It was not an unpleasant feeling.

"Hello?" she whispered, glancing around to confirm that she was, indeed, alone. She felt a bit foolish but it had taken her ages to work up the nerve. "Is … is anyone there?"

Lysander wheeled herself closer still to The Barrel;

she was now flush with the base. No weeds or grass came even close to touching it. Clearly, Mr. Peabody took his job very seriously. Taking a deep breath, she stretched out her fingers. Mature beyond her years, she would have denied her fear at that very moment, but her tiny hand trembled all the same.

It was warm and smooth. Her fingers tingled.

THEY WILL COME. TIME GROWS SHORT. YOU MUST PREPARE.

She gasped and her hand dropped to her lap.

"Who said that?!" she demanded, though she knew the voice had spoken only in her head.

"Who said what?" came a gruff voice from behind her. "You shouldn't be that close to it you know!"

Walter Peabody shuffled slowly up beside her. Lysander swallowed nervously, expecting to be in trouble: Mr. Peabody was notoriously protective of The Barrel.

"Sorry sir. I …"

"Did you touch The Barrel?"

She nodded reluctantly, chagrined.

He sighed. "Did it talk to you? Tell me the truth now!"

Lysander's eyes widened. All she could do was nod.

Walter scratched his grizzled chin. "*The child will lead the way.*" He said as he regarded her through narrowed eyes. "That's what it told me back in '61 when I touched it myself. 'Spose that's you. Been waitin'."

Lysander stared, opened mouthed.

"Quit yer gaping girl. See what else it has to say."

And so, hand placed firmly on the surface of The Barrel, Lysander relayed a long list of instructions to Walter.

He dutifully and neatly transcribed them into a small notebook he kept in the front pocket of his shirt. By the time Amelia Drake returned to the square, punnet of strawberries in hand, Walter was long gone; a sense of urgency in his step. He had much to do over the next few days.

Back at home, Lysander pondered how to explain everything to her mother. She wheeled herself into the kitchen where Amelia was preparing a salad for dinner.

"Mummy … we need to talk."

***

A pregnant summer moon hung low and heavy in the early morning sky as a ragtag assortment of characters made their way to the center of town. Dawn was still several hours away. They came to a stop in the square, gathering around The Barrel. There were not as many as Lysander had hoped – her mother, Mr. Peabody, the Sherman's and their young twins; Dr. Aiden Folpp; Brenda Okpik and Clary Freemont, both nurses; Farmer Ted and a few others who had been convinced by the earnestness of Lysander and Walter's story. There were just twenty-two of them.

It was time. Lysander and Walter approached The Barrel, looked at each other and nodded. Simultaneously they placed their hands on the sleek, silver surface. Almost at once a strange faint whirring sound reached their ears; the object emitted a warm ethereal glow that soon enveloped its custodians. Amelia Drake gasped and, though her hand reached out for her daughter, she did not touch her.

Then, abruptly, it stopped.

Lysander and Walter smiled and turned to face the small gathering.

"It's ready."

Behind them, a low rumble arose and the ground quaked beneath their feet. Wary but consumed with curiosity, they craned their necks for a glimpse of what might happen next. The children clung to their parent's legs and watched on in wide-eyed wonder as an opening appeared in The Barrel. A door. A small ramp slid forward; Walter looked to Lysander for permission and once granted, he placed his hands on the handles of her chair and began to push her up the ramp.

"Follow us!" she called, her face radiant with joy.

Amelia trailed her daughter up the ramp, the others behind her in succession, stepping into the darkness beyond… and what would be their salvation.

***

A day passed. And then a week. An entire year, almost to the day had passed, when things upon the surface finally went awry.

In those twelve months' prior, the townspeople had patted themselves on the back for not falling for the lies of Lysander Drake and Walter Peabody. Nothing had happened. A complete fabrication. They called them false prophets and other things that could not be repeated in polite company.

When the morning of July 20th rolled around, it was expected to be an ordinary day like any other.

Until it wasn't.

The first blast hit a hillside on the outskirts of town around 9am. Farmer Ted's homestead and pasture, abandoned the year before, was completely obliterated. A large smoking crater took its place. It sent the residents into a full fledged panic.

At 9:13 am an explosion rocked the east side of town. What wasn't immediately cremated, erupted in flames. As ashes fell from the sky like snow, people could be seen fleeing towards the town square. They pounded upon the surface of The Barrel, begging and screaming until they were hoarse.

What followed was a series of well orchestrated strikes that left Fabrishermshire smoldering in ruins.

When the noise had settled, The Barrel could be heard emitting a series of sharp beeps – if there had been anyone left there to hear it that is. Smoothly, it descended into the ground. A small dimple in the dirt the only record that anything had ever been there.

When the first alien ship landed and its inhabitants set foot upon the Earth, they appeared quite pleased with their achievements. No one would have understood the language that they spoke but if they had, they would have learned that there'd been no real purpose behind the destruction. They had done it simply because they could. They collected a few human bones as a souvenir but otherwise, they didn't stay for very long. There was more fun to be had elsewhere on this planet.

***

Perhaps one day, when the lands are once again habitable, The Barrel will rise and a new town square will rise around it.

After all, history does have a way of repeating itself.

HOW TALL THE TREES HAD GROWN

Giulia watched with childlike wonder, enchanted as the snow continued to fall throughout the day. This was to be expected Mother said, the climate had shifted again. As the winds whipped into a frenzy Giulia was called away from the window, made to join her family as they huddled near the fire. The heat brought life back to her chilled limbs and she gave thanks that Father had well stocked the hearth before the storms arrival.

They could no longer see out the window.

That night they read by candlelight, ate venison stew and did their best to ignore the tempest howling outside. They slept together beneath piles of patchwork quilts.

There was a stillness to the air when they arose in the morning. And thus began the difficult process of digging their way out. Using spoons, cups and bowls, Giulia and her siblings scooped and tossed, enjoying their first taste of cold weather. Their fingers were nearly blue as they broke through to the surface.

Her cloak trailing behind her as she ran, Giulia was the first to reach the tree. She stretched a hand out tentatively, experimentally, breathing deeply of the scent of fresh snow and pine.

"It melts!" Arlo exclaimed of the snow.

"Yes, Father says it will bring back our rivers," Giulia whispered, voice reverent.

The trees had grown so tall over the years, that she could not remember a time when they did not soar towards the sun.

Behemoths now buried, nearly to the top.

THE MARKET

"We shouldn't be talking!"

"Do you think he could change his mind?"

"They never do, darling, they never do. Now go!"

***

It was barely dawn, but Cherish Watson had already undertaken a day's work. The house was spotless and she was feeling accomplished; soon she would drop the children at school and then she would be free to spend the rest of the day as she pleased. She was planning to make an apple cobbler for dessert tonight which meant a special trip across town to the farmer's market for Granny Smiths. It was Desmond's favorite though, so she would find the time.

She heard tiny but thunderous feet hit the floor above her head signaling the end of her solitude, and as she pulled bowls and spoons for oatmeal from their respective cupboards and drawers, Lucas and Delilah exploded into the kitchen. She shook her head wearily at their bickering but turned away to hide a grin. Even in the womb they hadn't been able to get along; always fighting and kicking for their own space. They inhaled their breakfast, then turned and smiled the exact same smile at her, before rushing off to brush their teeth. She felt a familiar stab of pain in her chest as the thought flashed in her mind of what life would be like without them; every mother's greatest fear.

With Lucas and Delilah safely delivered to school later, Cherish made the trek to the market for apples. She found herself unable to resist the seductive scent of fresh bread wafting from the bakery as she strolled past. She grabbed a baguette and hurried on her way, her allowance card depleted for the day. She paused a few doors down to chat briefly with a new neighbor, leaning against the white picket fence to compliment the roses in the garden. And then, determined to finish the book she was reading, she made a beeline for home, retrieving it from its hiding spot behind a bag of peas in the freezer. With cobbler crisping in the oven, she poured herself a generous glass of pilfered red, and slipped beneath the bubbles of a hot bath.

The water had long grown cold by the time she closed the book. She pulled the plug in the tub with her toes, quickly towelled herself dry and tidied the bathroom. She chose a favorite blue sundress from the closet. She'd been told that it complemented her eyes. She curled her hair so that it fell in soft waves to the middle of her back and expertly applied just the right amount of makeup.

At last, content with her appearance, she padded barefoot to the kitchen, which was now resplendent with the smells of cinnamon and cloves. She swept a discerning eye over the room, wiped an errant crumb from the countertop but otherwise could spot nothing out of place. It was perfect.

She shooed the kids to their rooms when they arrived from school a little later and set the table with the special occasion china. Moroccan lamb tagine with lemon and pomegranate couscous now perfumed the air. She had outdone herself this time and gave herself a mental pat on the back. She could be convincing if she had to be. She knew all it took was one phone call.

Desmond arrived home later than usual, flustered but with an apologetic bouquet of her favorite flowers. She placed the daisies in the center of the table and stood back to admire her handy work. This should be on the cover of a magazine, she thought and then laughed out loud, sharply, startling herself.

Deep breaths. Calming breaths. Composure. She smiled brightly at nothing in particular and shouted, "Dinner's ready!"

***

It had gone well. The day was almost over. She was optimistic. Desmond was upstairs supervising the children's bath time. They were boisterous and noisy, their father's indulgent voice doing little to settled them down. She was putting away the leftovers, neatly labeled with reheating instructions, when she heard a noise above the commotion upstairs. The low rumble as it came around the corner was familiar and unmistakable, and she knew now that it was too late.

There was a screech and huff of the air brakes as it pulled up out front, then the idling of the engine. The Recycling Truck. Then, a knock on the door. She hesitated, her hands stilling on the refrigerator. What would happen if she simply didn't answer?

Just by chance she had seen the catalogue addressed to Desmond arrive in the mail a month ago. It had disappeared into his office very quickly but, by then, she'd known that he was shopping around. She had hoped, had tried her best to be the perfect wife… But she should have known better.

Disappointment swamped her and she wiped her suddenly sweaty palms down the sides of her dress before forcing herself to walk to the door. There was no other option.

"Good evening, ma'am. Having reached the end of the thirty-day notice period as required from your current leaseholder, I hereby inform you that under the authority of The Depot … "

Cherish had stopped listening. She nodded once, accepting his words, and stepped outside. She'd heard it all before of course and knew the drill by now. Still, she couldn't help glancing back at the house as she walked away, thinking of the children. Not just the twins, but remembering all the little ones who had come before them.

She wished she could stay or at least, just once, have a chance to say goodbye.

Tomorrow they would have a new mommy. And she would be back on the market.

THE GODDESS OF THE FOUR WINDS

On the cusp of creation, the Goddess sent a Raja to each of the four winds. Chosen for their ability to rule with a fair and moral hand, she bestowed upon each of them their own sacred corner of Mother Earth; the point where the divine graces the natural world. For centuries there was peace, the factions thrived, and she was pleased.

But then came The Great Dissent; greed and jealously became rampant, and wars arose among the conclaves. North, South, East and West were brought to their knees: divided and conquered. This angered the Goddess and thus, to appease her, an armistice was reluctantly declared. The Goddess loved her people deeply and so she spared them, despite their wicked ways. In exchange for her mercy it was decreed that each year, on the summer solstice, they would all gather in celebration, to give thanks and rejoice.

A hundred years had come to pass. There had been countless times throughout the ages when only her intervention had prevented a downward spiral into complete chaos … for as is wont to happen sometimes with humans, even when they are satisfied, they always want just a little bit more.

The music is lively as this year's festivities begin. There is laughter and spirits are high, but beneath all this, the seeds of discord have once again been sown. The Goddess, having grown tired, watches from afar knowing another battle is on the horizon. She nods then, decisively: this will be the end.

THE LAST ONE STANDING

She could remember a time when the sun still shone; when she was small, and a cool, crisp breeze on an autumn day was something she could selfishly take for granted. Before the storms came.

The rain began on an ordinary day, but by the end of the week, when it continued to fall, it felt anything but. The winds lashed with cruel purpose. Buildings were leveled, and homes destroyed. Rising flood waters overwhelmed bridges, and they inevitably succumbed to the waves. Global temperatures plummeted, and a panic descended on the world; the few who were able to endure the weather had far worse things to worry about.

When they found her, she was alone, sheltered beneath the battered bows of a half-fallen oak. And they marvelled at her survival.

Her arrival at the facility was met with much enthusiasm. The scientists hurried to examine her: they took samples, there were endless tests, and she was poked and prodded until finally they allowed her some peace. Safe within their artificial light and their artificial oxygen, she came to the scariest realization of all: they had known, they had been prepared for this.

So, the years went by and unwittingly it became home. She grew; somehow she flourished, while outside, in a world gone mad, infrastructure and humanity crumbled. She heard rumours of rising factions amongst the few who had survived out there, for the leaders spoke around her freely, her silence mistaken for indifference. There was talk of one-day re-terraforming and repopulating. She was told she would be instrumental in this of course: the revival of the earth.

They had so much to learn from her. The last of her kind. The last tree.

FAR OUT

Nose pressed against the window, I gazed with unconcealed interest as my fellow travelers bid tearful goodbyes to their loved ones out on the tarmac. I had already boarded eagerly; the first to do so. I was leaving nothing behind that was worth crying about. I only felt relief.

I sat back in my seat, secured my harness, and gaped in wide eyed wonder at my surroundings. Everything was high-tech, polished and ultra-modern, and though I hated to admit it, most was far beyond my comprehension.

I was still shocked to be here. Me, Audrey Melrose, sitting aboard the Madonna 61. The much-hyped civilian inhabited spaceship would be the first of its kind to travel to another planet. It was a technological marvel, and everyone wanted in on it. The manifest bore names of some of the world's top scientists and experts in the fields of astronomy, biology, and terraformation. No expense had been spared, and like anything done on such a grand scale, the expedition needed more and more money to get off the ground. Consequently, a few thrillseeker celebrities, and at least one professional athlete, had been able to buy their way on board. But everyone else was ordinary like me. A streetwise foster kid who had just aged out of the system, plucked from obscurity and thrust into the spotlight; my name randomly chosen by an automated system along with 159 others.

We were about to make history.

***

We had known our world was dying long before the authorities finally acknowledged it, but by then it was too little, too late. In order to save our species, they had to set their sights farther than ever before... to the stars. Surely ours wasn't the only planet capable of supporting life. Time was fast running out when they finally made a breakthrough and by then, relocating was the obvious, and only, solution for survival.

Shortly after we had been notified of our selection and had passed all the requisite physical and psychological examinations, we were taken on an extensive tour of the ship. It was thrilling but just impossible to take it all in. I had been assigned a small anchored pod on one of the lower levels and, given my poor social skills, I expected that I would spend much of my time there. The accommodations were stark and white: a small room with nothing more than a bunk, a small built in bookshelf, and a desk with a chair. I overheard a few mumbled under-the-breath complaints at the simplicity and lack of comforts, but I was thrilled to have something that was all mine. It was not lavish by any means, no, but it was clean and safe and warm, which was more than I could have said for most of my foster homes. It even had a tiny window: my very own personal planetarium.

***

I watched openly now as the others embarked. We were "a broad cross section of society" they had exclaimed at the orientation and, yes, it certainly seemed as though we represented all walks of life. It had also been announced, with much fanfare, that as an added incentive we would receive education and training in a field of our choice as we journeyed through space. Upon our arrival there, we would be expected to use the skills we had learned en route to help establish the first settlement, so that others could eventually follow. It was exhilarating but overwhelming to be a part of something so huge.

Now here we were, the moment we'd been waiting for: launch day. There was a tense excitement in the air. We could feel that we were perched on the precipice of something magnificent, and there was no going back. There was uneasy chatter, bursts of nervous laughter and the worriers – there were quite a few -- anxiously poured over the information packages we'd found on our seats. I picked up my envelope and ran a finger along the flap to open it. I pulled out the hefty bundle of papers and sifted through them absently. Satellite photos of our destination spilled across my lap – my first look – and I stared in stunned silence. This was going to be my new home.

"Good morning all! Welcome aboard the Madonna 61!"

As the applause died down, I shifted my focus to the steward who would now instruct us as we prepped for flight.

"… you are tutelaries of the new world, giving hope to all those left behind. Your dedication and sacrifice have not gone unnoticed. And so today you will embark upon a journey of infinite possibilities! Destination: Earth."

ON SALE NOW FROM ENGEN BOOKS

THE SIX ELEMENTAL

ALI HOUSE

The myth of the Six-Elemental is almost seven hundred years old, and the possibility of someone having the power of more than one Element has been thoroughly disproven by science. None of this matters, however, when Kit Tyler receives the power of all six Elements on her twenty-first birthday.

"Blending the worlds of science and mythology, The Six Elemental is a compelling page-turner with a heroine we can all relate to."
Amanda Labonté, author of *Call of the Sea*

Also available: *The Fifth Queen* by Ali House

ON SALE NOW FROM ENGEN BOOKS

"Dunne breathes life into a world of magic and lore that will draw the reader in right up to the epic conclusion. Ashes is a heroic tale not to be missed."
Amanda Labonté
bestselling author of Supenatural Causes

When fifteen-year-old Phoenix loses her caregiver, everyone that she has ever known inexplicably turn their backs on her. Given the impossible burden of repaying an unknown debt, Phoenix sets out on her own with her trusty donkey, Muler, as her only companion.A chance encounter with Malcourt, a mysterious traveller, not only saves her life, but sets it on a trajectory that she would have never thought possible.

ON SALE NOW FROM ENGEN BOOKS

HEED THE CALL

After a heated fight at sea between twins Ben and Alex, Ben vanishes from their boat without a sound or even a ripple in the water. Unwavering in his dedication to find his brother, Alex begins the adventure of a lifetime armed only with the help of a local girl named Meg and his own mysterious musical abilities… the key to which, and to the mysteries that surround him, may be tied to the alluring song of the dangerous girl he finds among the ocean's frothing waves.

"A mysterious figure in the ocean, a suspicious loss in the waves, a riveting treasure hunt, and surprise after surprise, how could anyone not want to read this novel?"

~Alice Kuipers
author of Life on the Refrigerator Door

"Loved this book and can't wait for the next one."

~Helen Escott
bestselling author of Operation: Wormwood

"It's been a while since I've read an entire book in one day, but…Whenever I tried to put it down, it would call out to me, luring me back like a siren's song."

~Ali House
author of The Six Elemental & The Fifth Queen

ABOUT THE AUTHOR

Nicole Little lives in St. John's. Her short stories have appeared in twelve anthologies thus far including five collections with Engen Books and seven collections from Australian publisher Black Hare Press. She has won several competitions including the June 2018 Kit Sora prize for her flash fiction piece "Sweet Sixteen;" her short story "Doxxed" placed 3rd in the Writers Alliance of Newfoundland and Labrador's "A Nightmare on Water Street: Scary Story Reading" in October 2018 and her three-sentence horror story, "Tasty Babies" earned her the much-coveted Hell Hare award from Black Hare Press in January 2020.

In her spare time, Nicole has either a pen in her hand or her nose in a book. She is married with two daughters.

The Lotus Fountain: A Slipstreamers Adventure is her first novella.

JD Ryot is the reclusive creator of the *Slipstreamers* series from Engen Books. JD is an avid fan of young adult literature and adventure serials.

www.ingramcontent.com/pod-product-compliance
Lightning Source LLC
Chambersburg PA
CBHW051951170626
46808CB00007B/2561